Cook Memorial Public Library

3 1122 01326 6112

FEB 1 2 2018

P9-DCC-697

The MANY DEATHS of SCOTT KOBLISH

The MANY DEATHS of SCOTT KOBLISH

By SCOTT KOBLISH

COOK MEMORIAL LIBRARY DISTRICT
413 N. MILWAUKEE AVE.
LIBERTYVILLE, ILLINOIS 60048

CHRONICLE BOOKS
SAN FRANCISCO

Copyright © 2018 by Scott Koblish. All Rights Reserved. No part of this book may be reproduced in any form without written permission form the publisher.

Library of Congress Cataloging-in-Publication Data

Names: Koblish, Scott, author, artist.
Title: The many deaths of Scott Koblish / by Scott Koblish.
Description: San Francisco : Chronicle Books, [2018]
Identifiers: LCCN 2017045090 | ISBN 9781452167121 (hardback)
Subjects: LCSH: American wit and humor, Pictorial. | Comic books, strips, etc. | BISAC: HUMOR / Form / Comic Strips & Cartoons.
Classification: LCC PN6727.K657 M36 2018 | DDC 741.5/973--dc23 LC record available at https://lccn.loc.gov/2017045090

Manufactured in China

Designed by Michael Morris

10 9 8 7 6 5 4 3 2

Chronicle Books LLC
680 Second Street
San Francisco, CA 94107
www.chroniclebooks.com

Chronicle Books publishes distinctive books and gifts. From award-winning children's titles, bestselling cookbooks, and eclectic pop culture to acclaimed works of art and design, stationery, and journals, we craft publishing that's instantly recognizable for its spirit and creativity. Enjoy our publishing and become part of our community at www.chroniclebooks.com.

THE BEAUTY OF NATURE

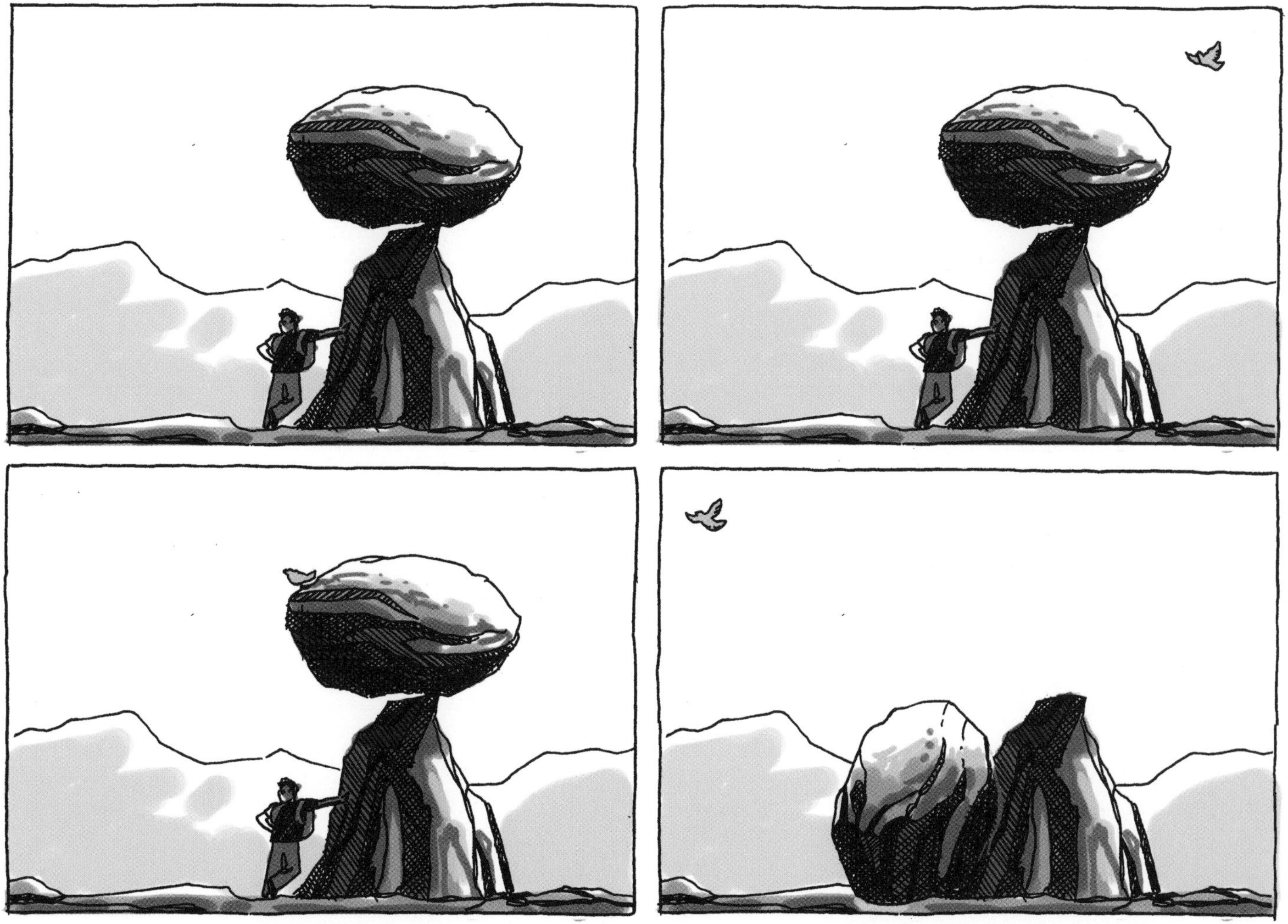

ALL DOWNHILL FROM HERE

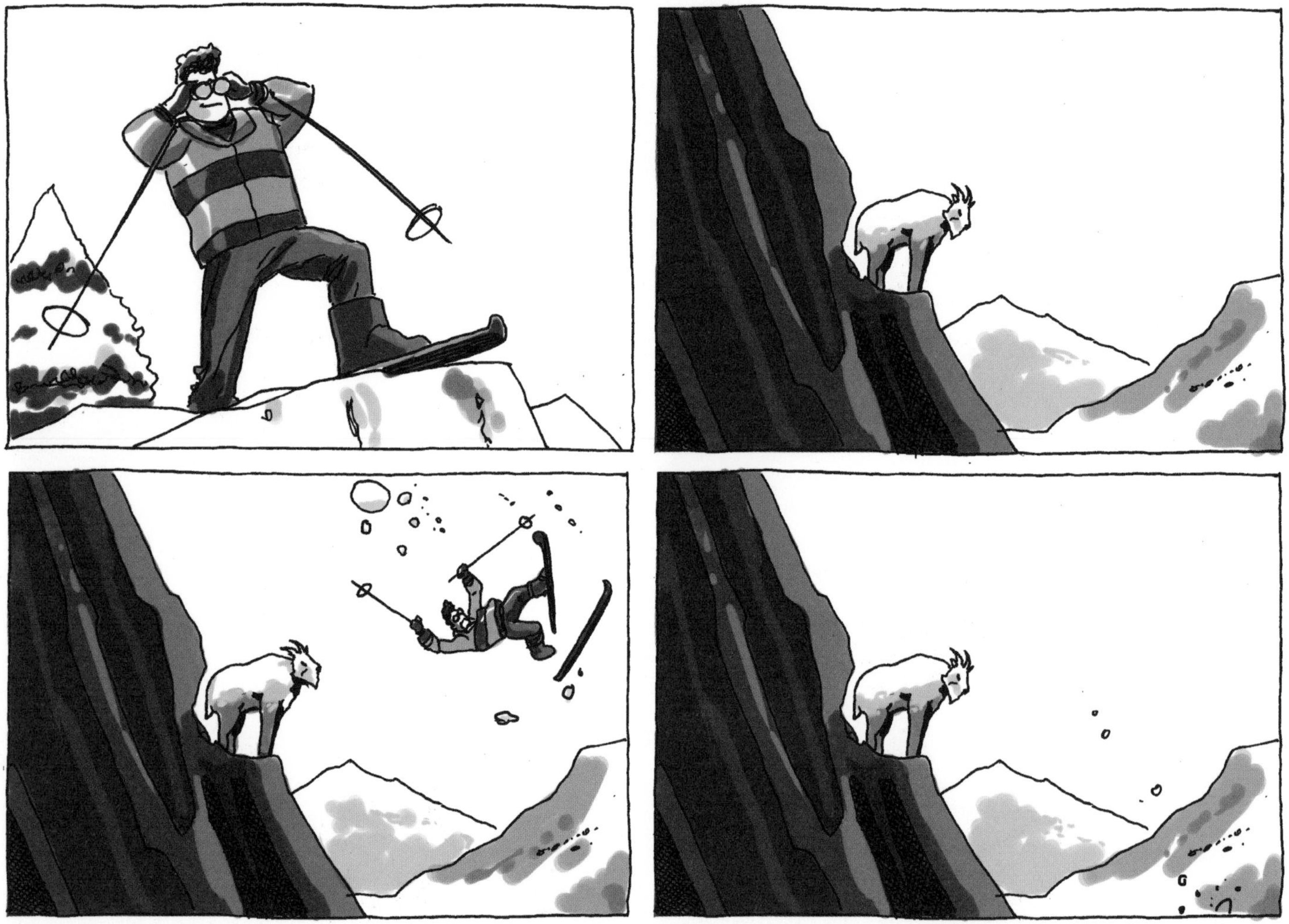

TGIF

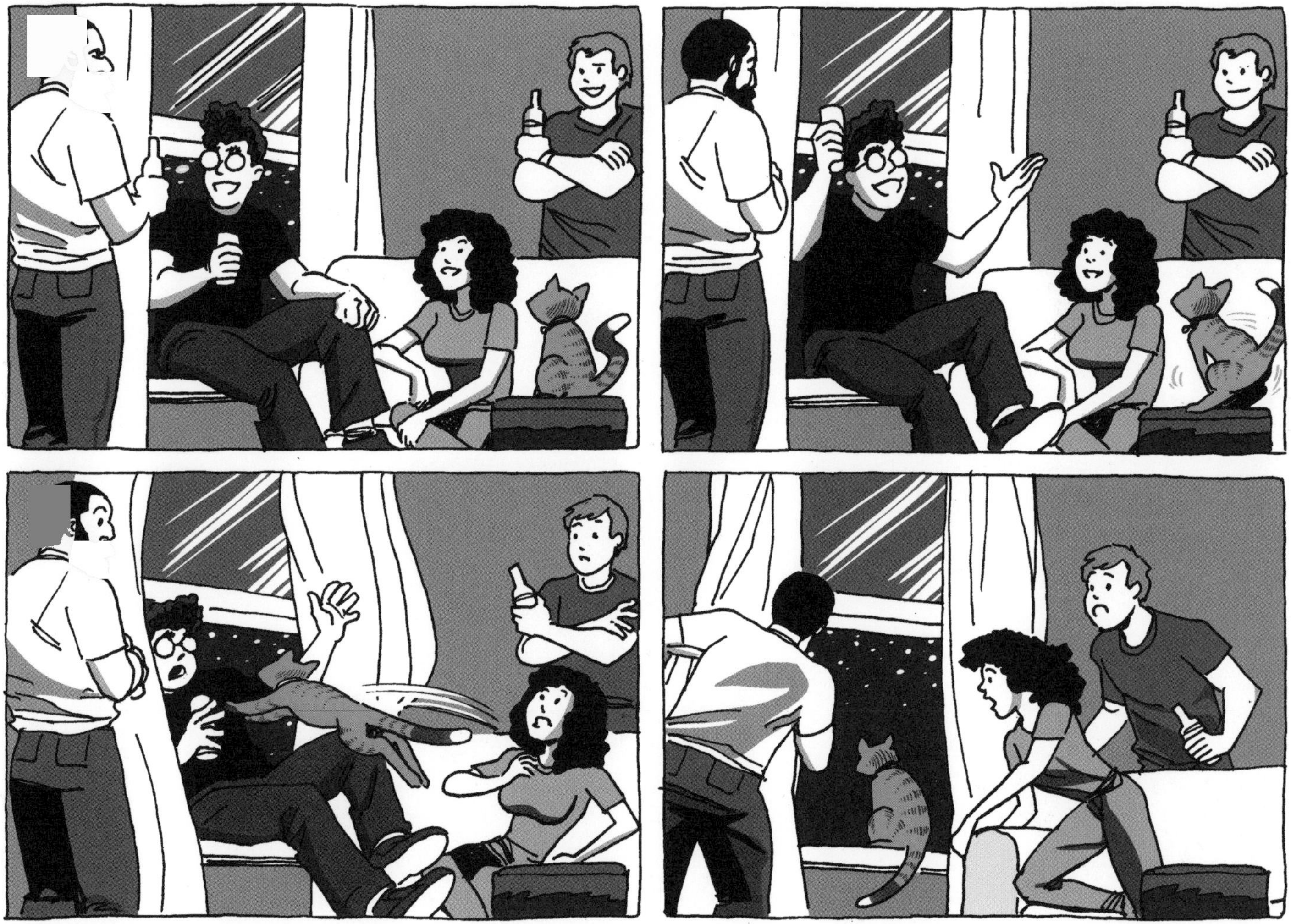

WHAT'S SHAKIN'?

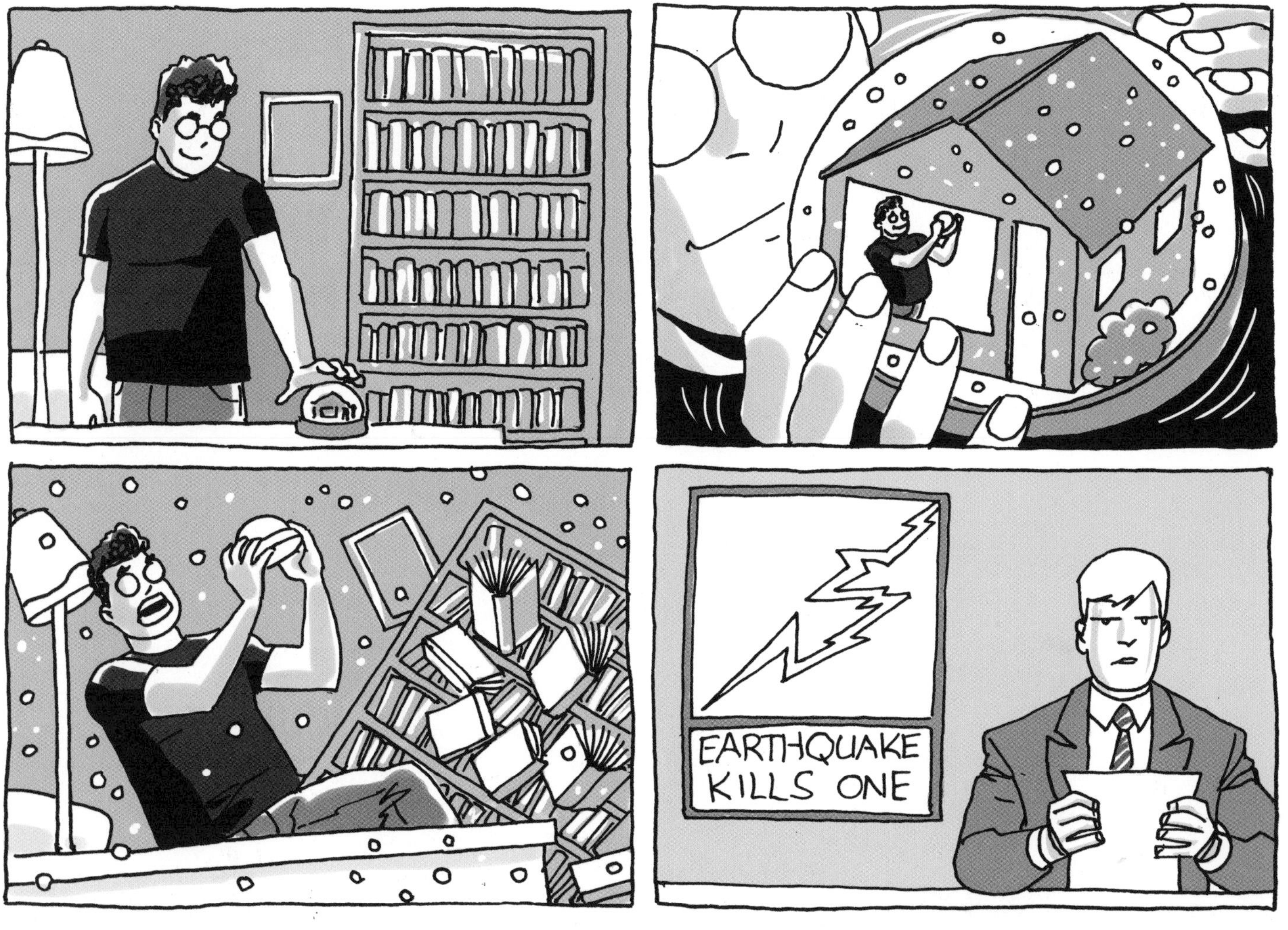
EARTHQUAKE
KILLS ONE

FINISHING TOUCHES

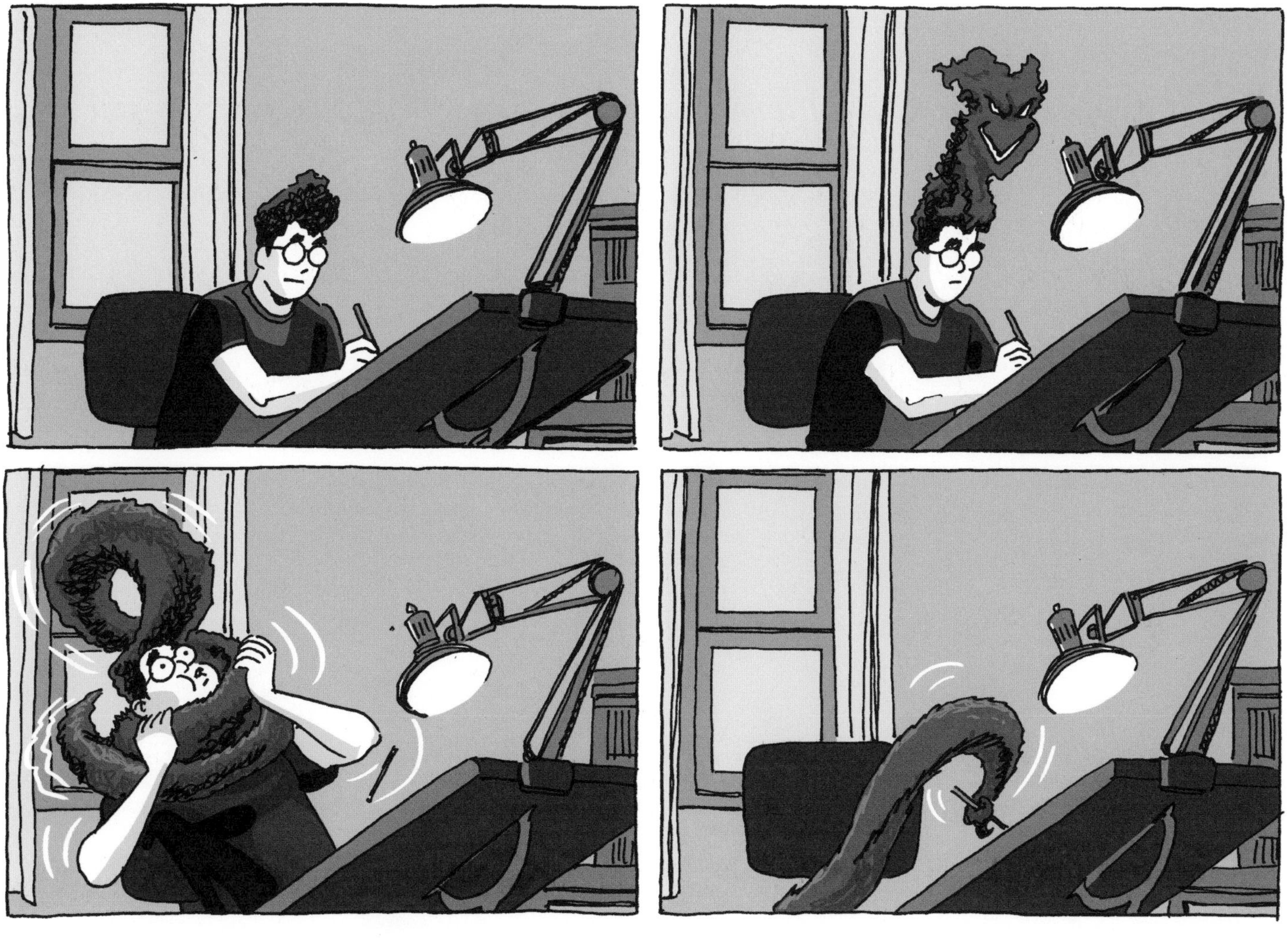

UP, UP, AND AWAY

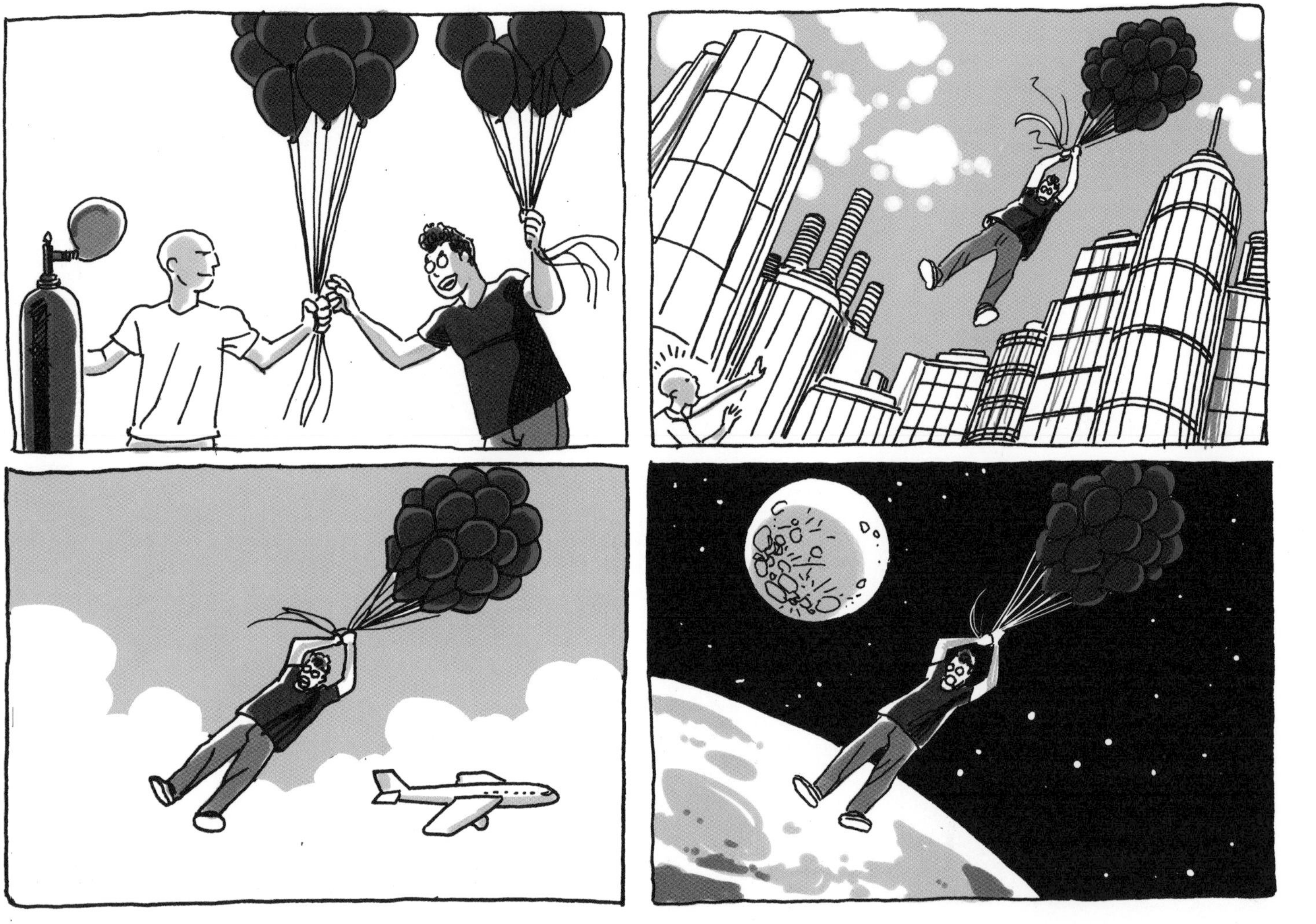

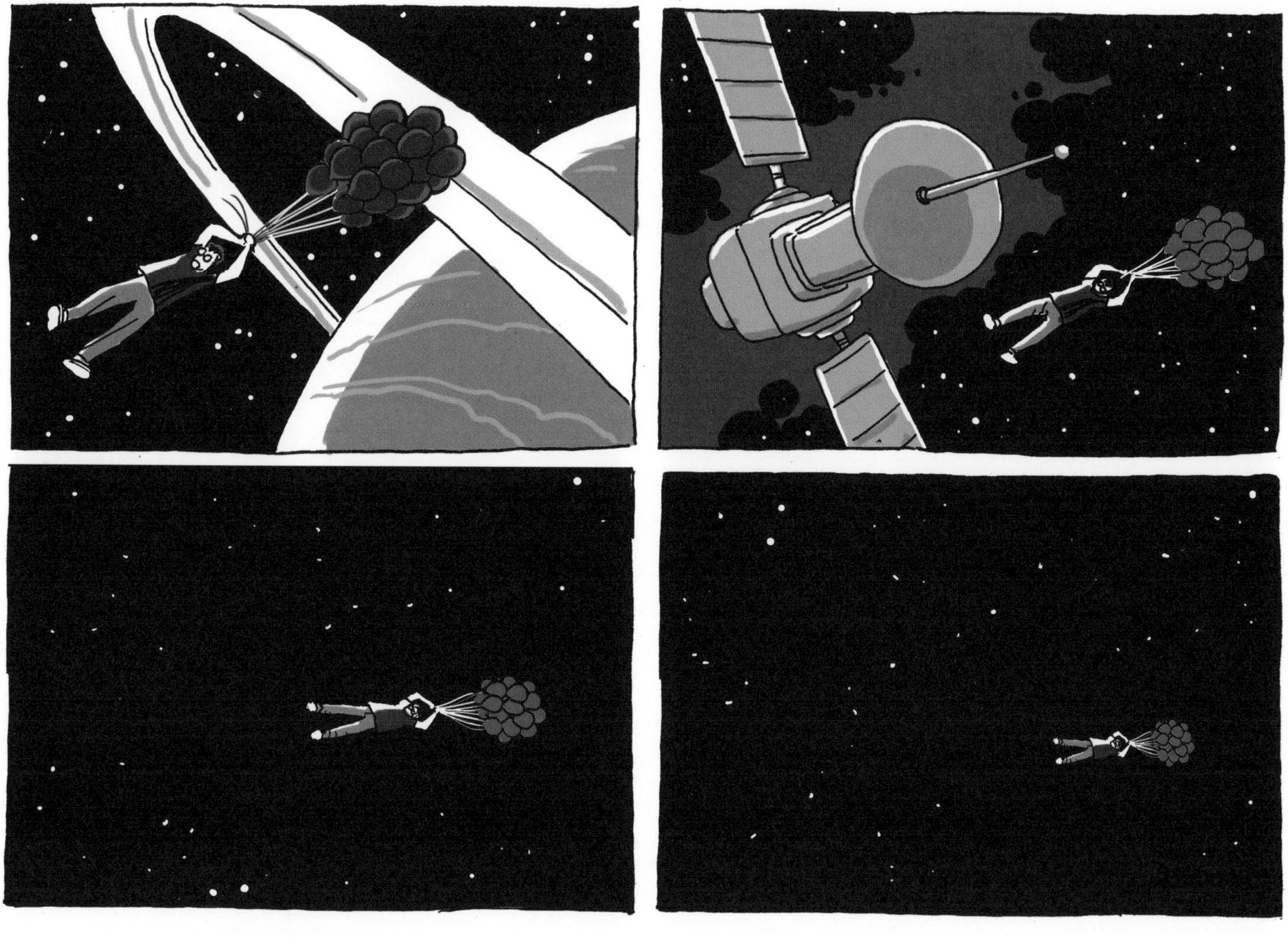

ONE UNREAD MESSAGE

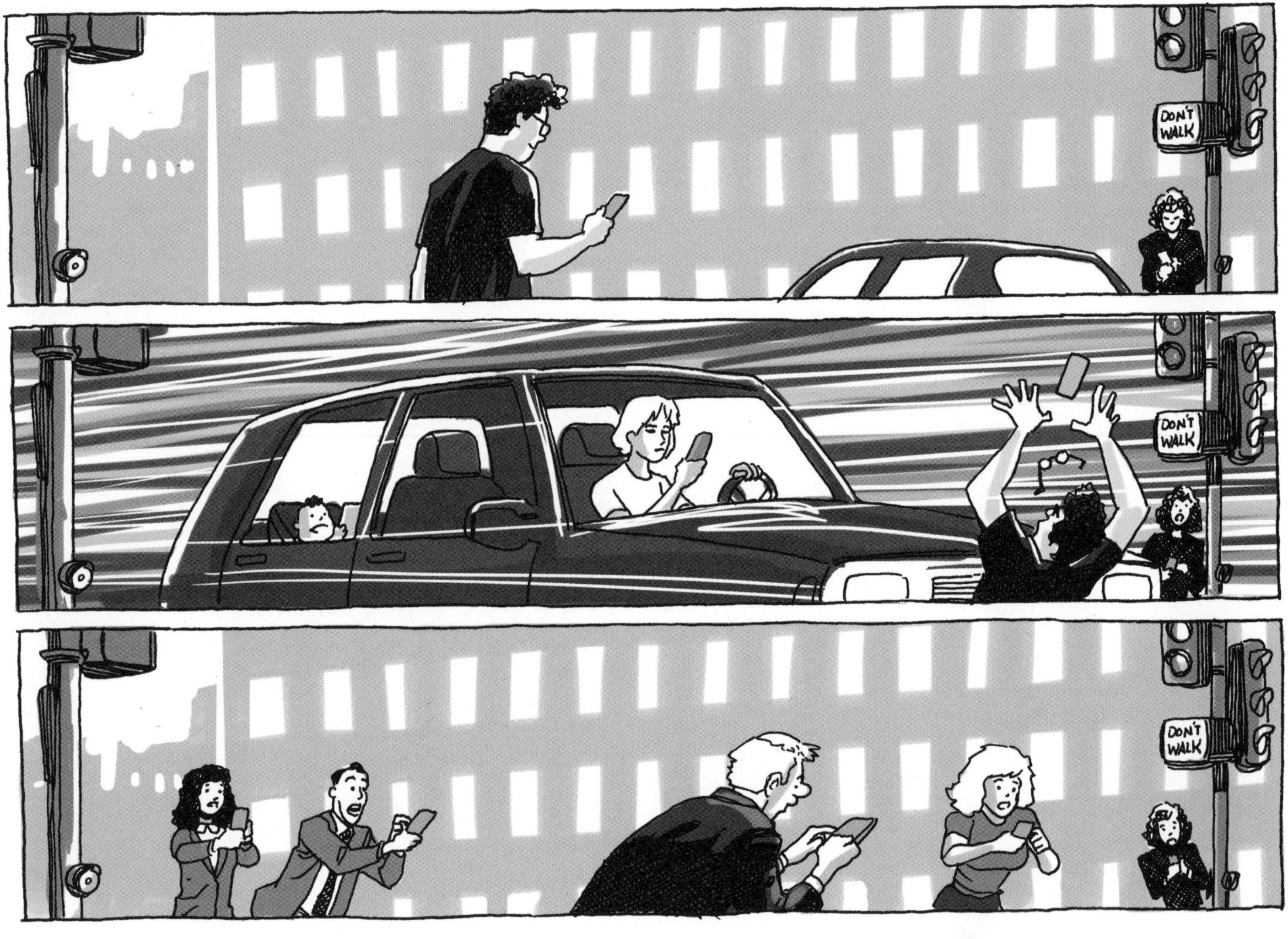

DON'T WALK
DON'T WALK
DON'T WALK

GOOD BOY

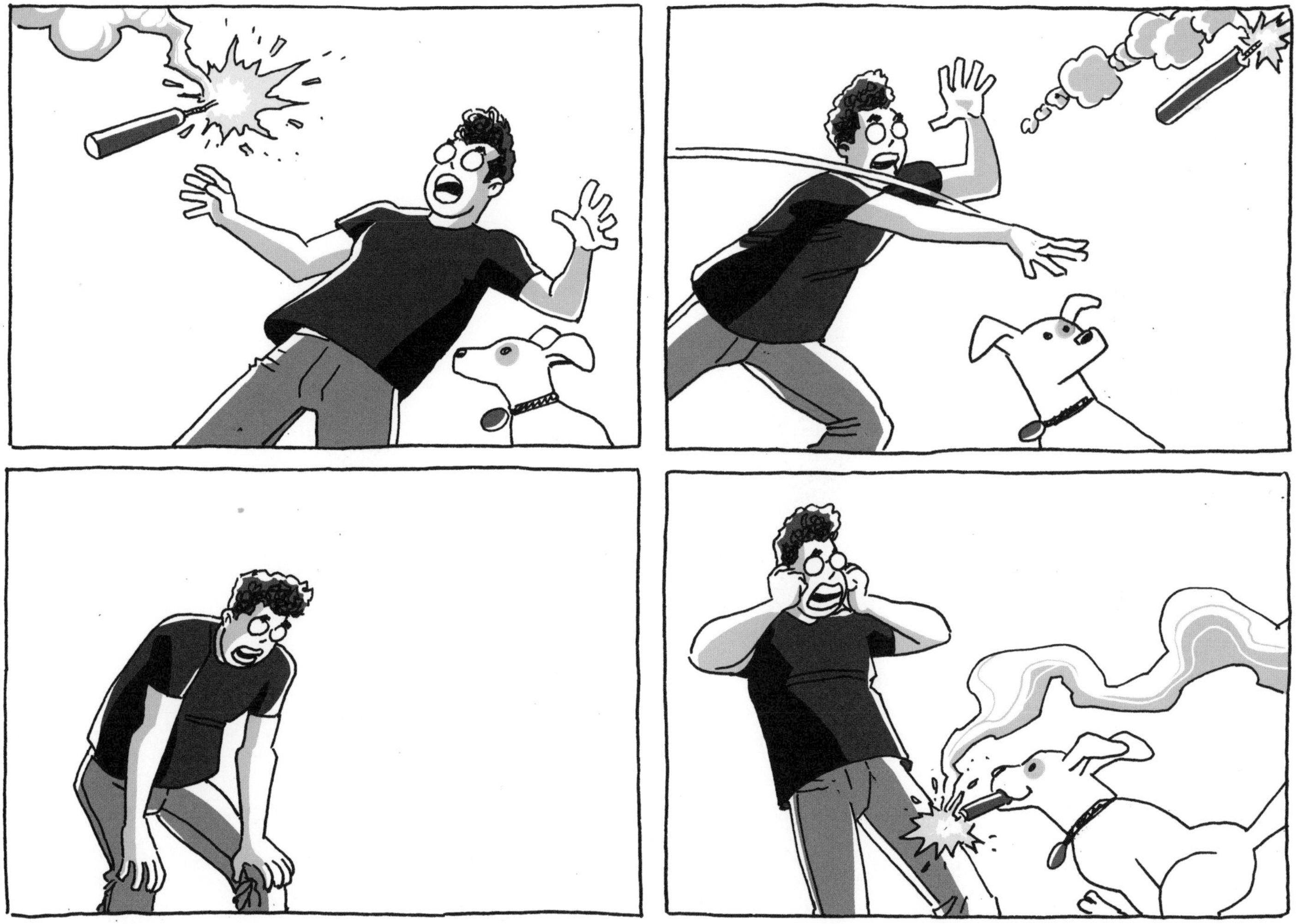

THE SCENIC ROUTE

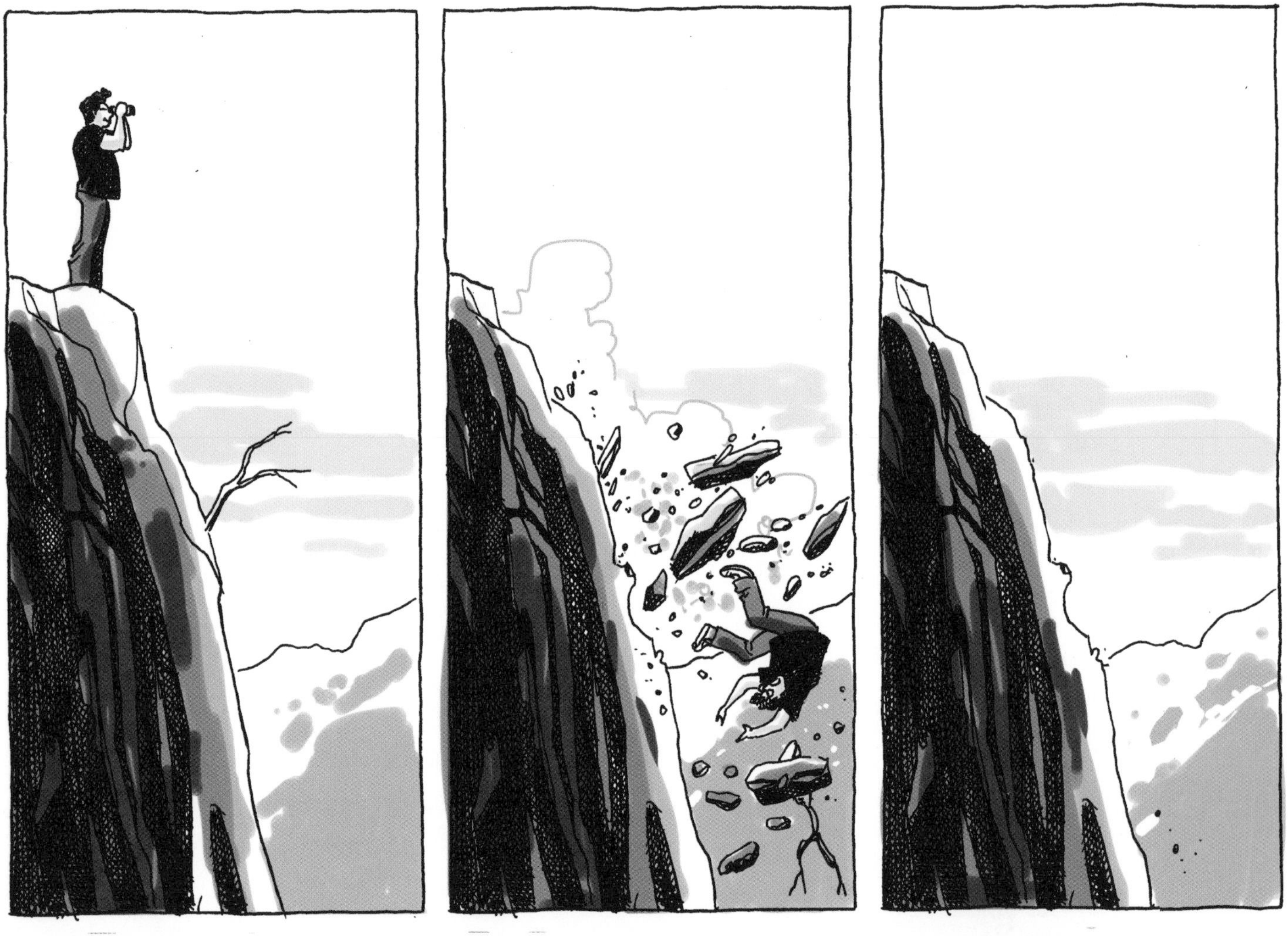

A DAY AT THE BEACH

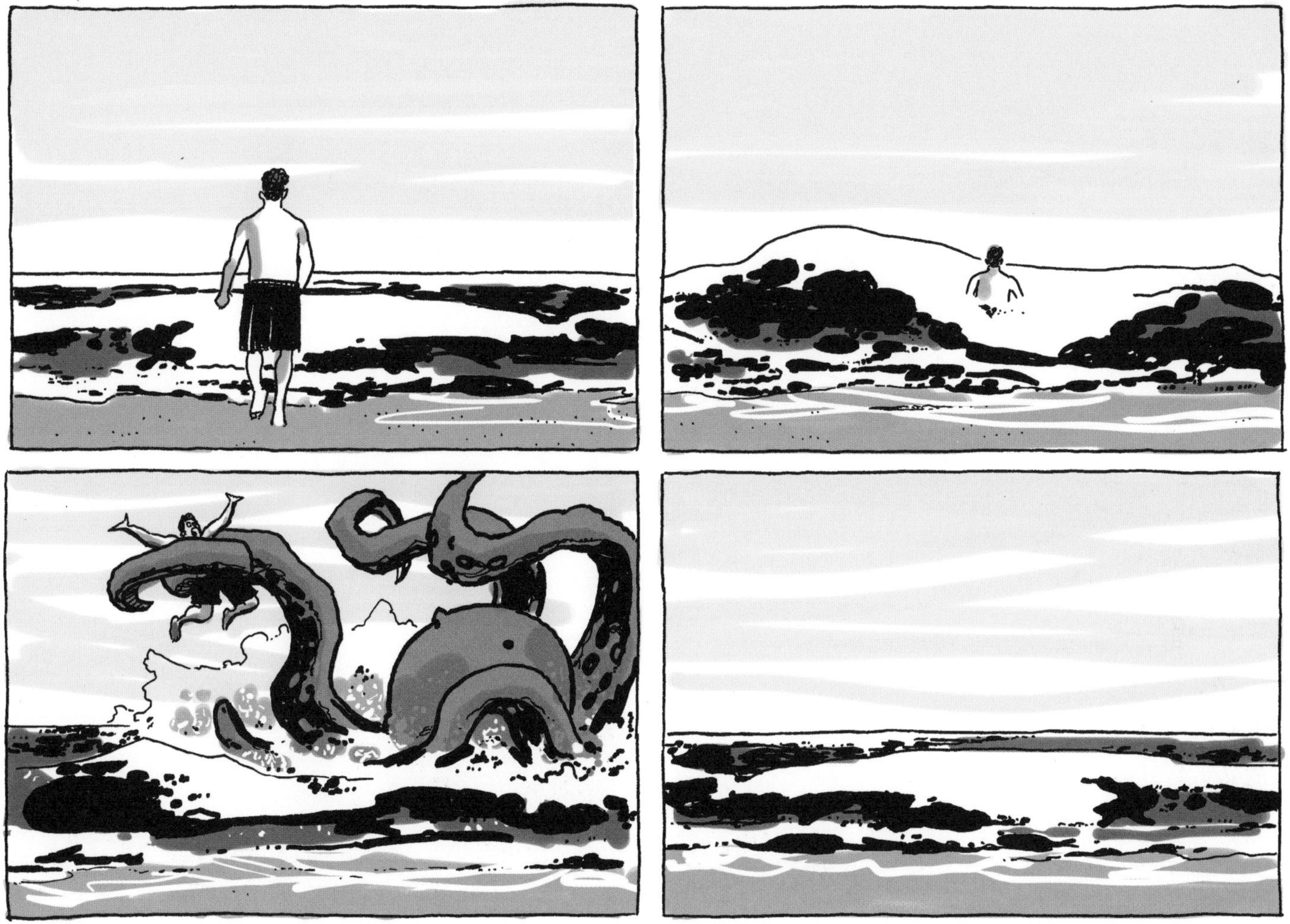

SO HORNY

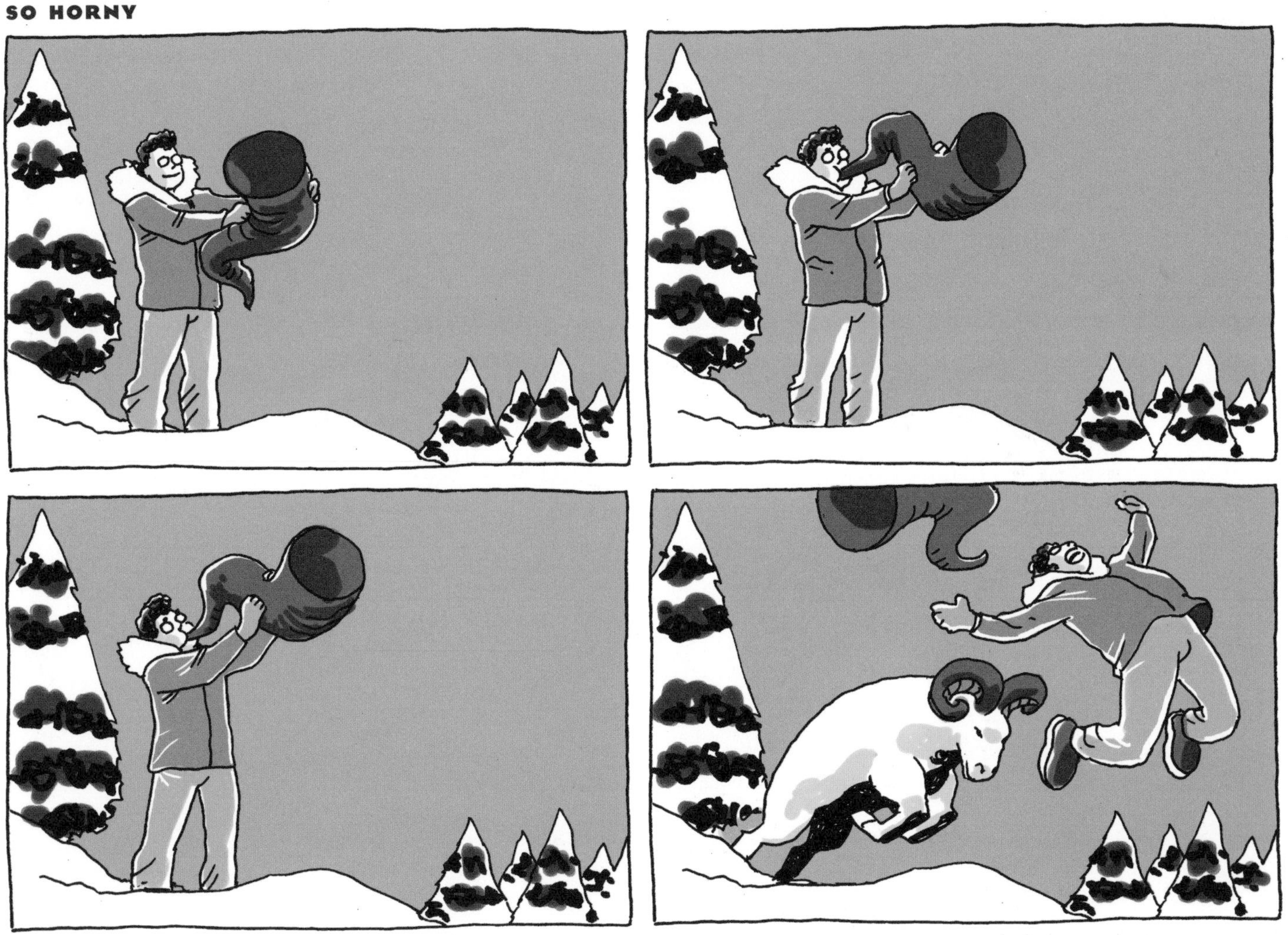

HISSY FIT

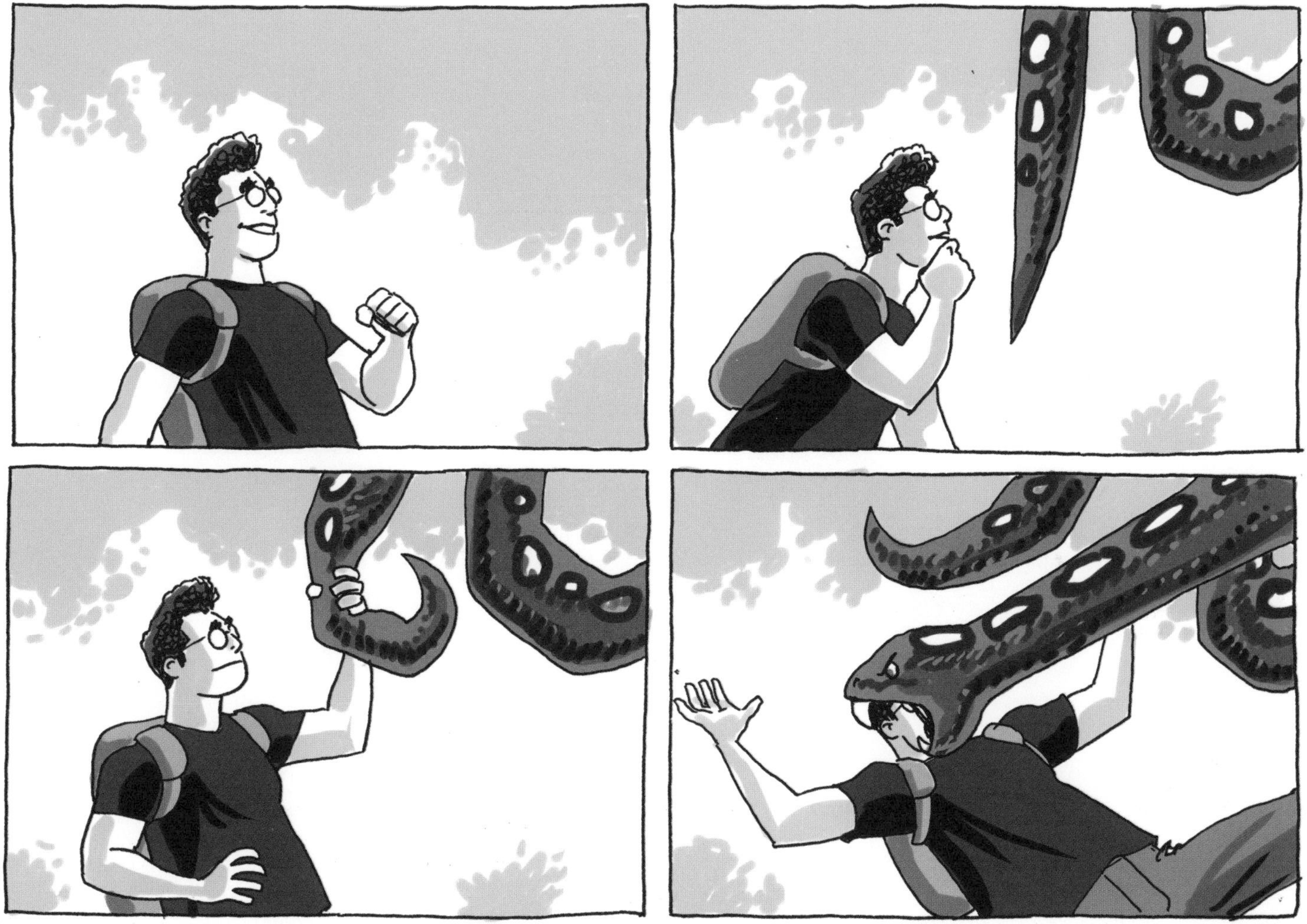

OH, THE HUGE MANATEE

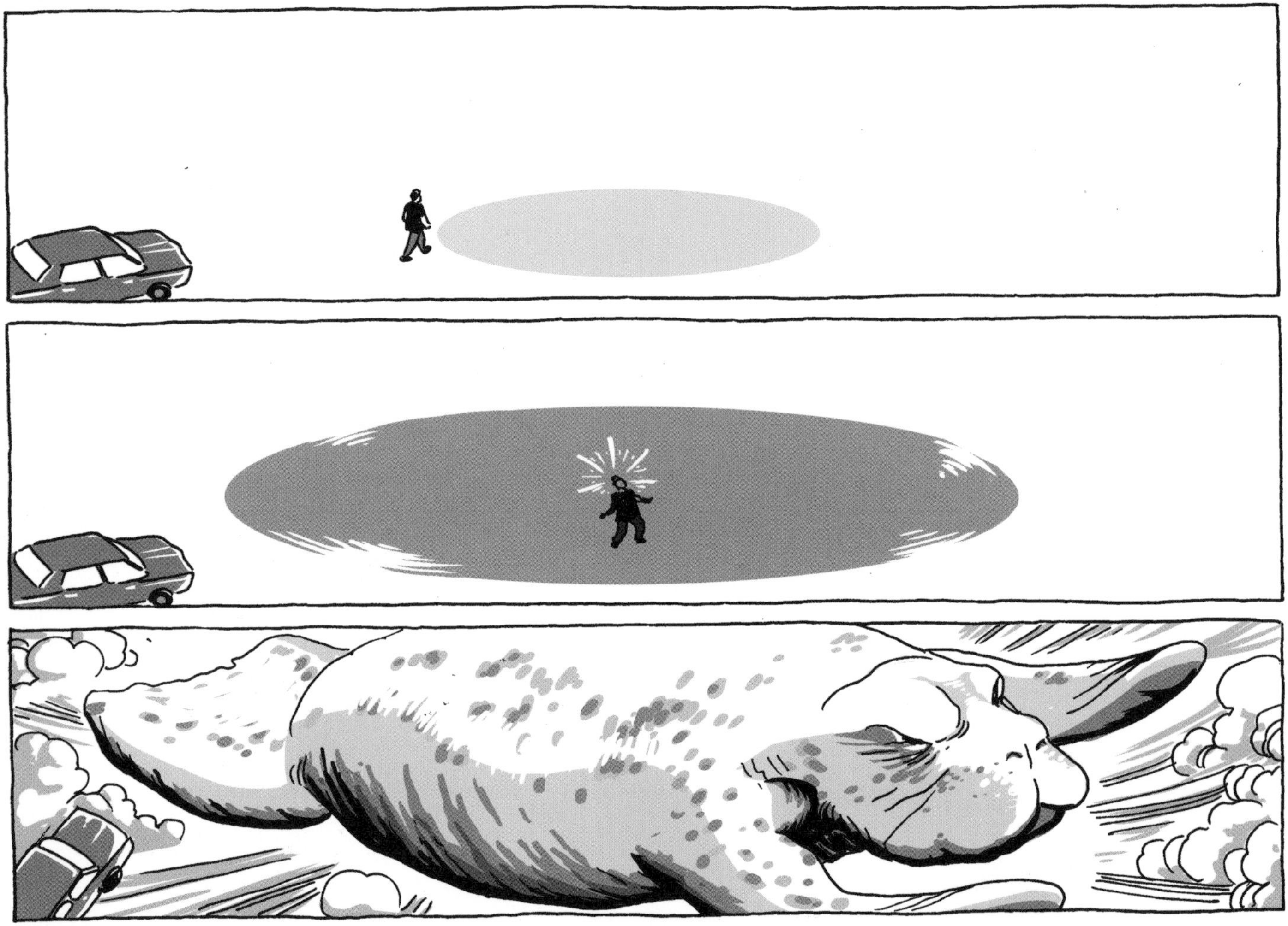

GONE FISHING

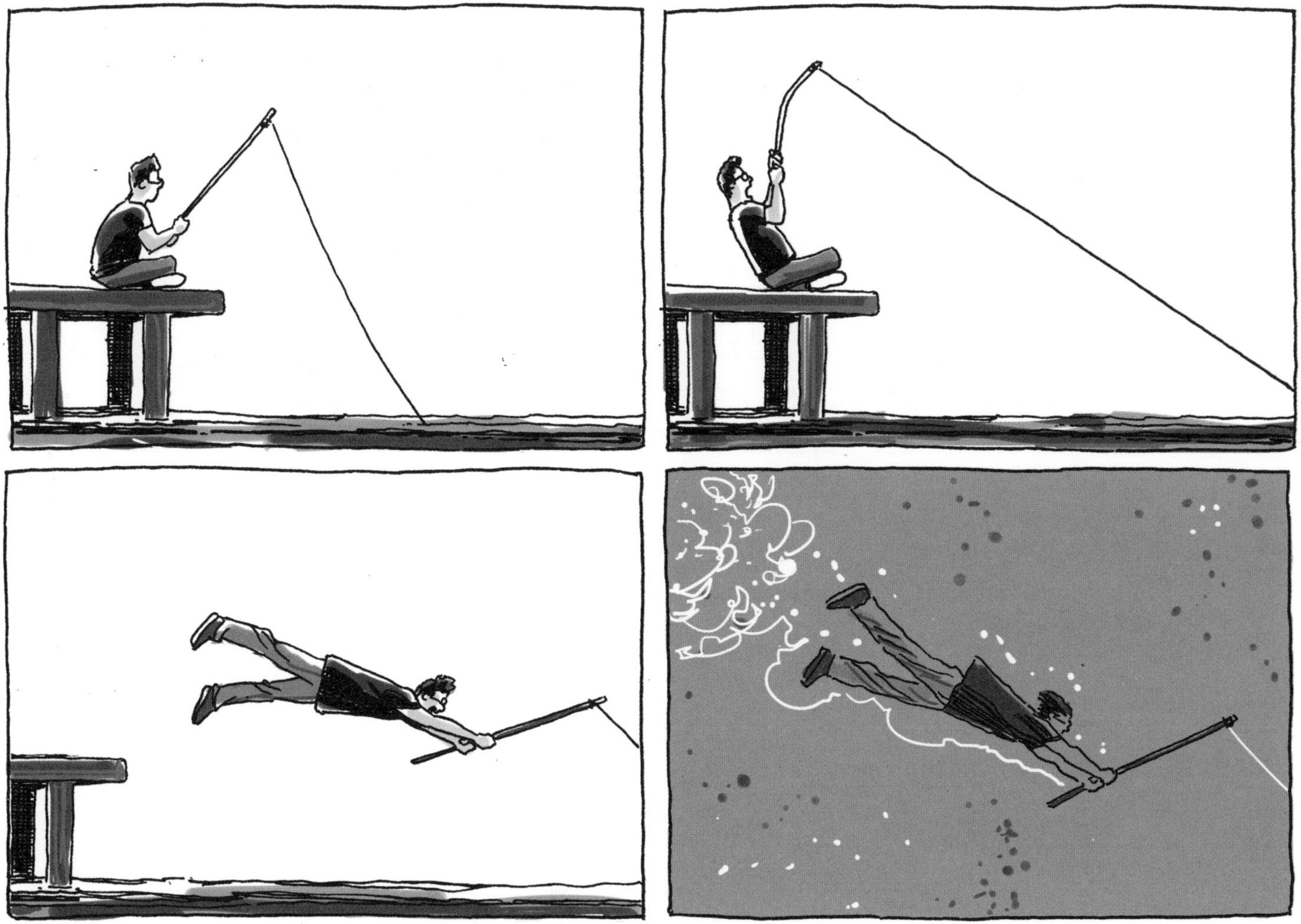

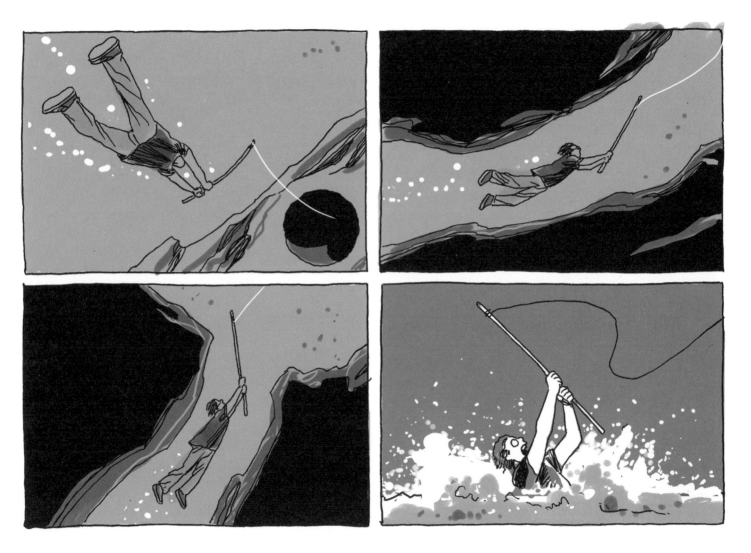

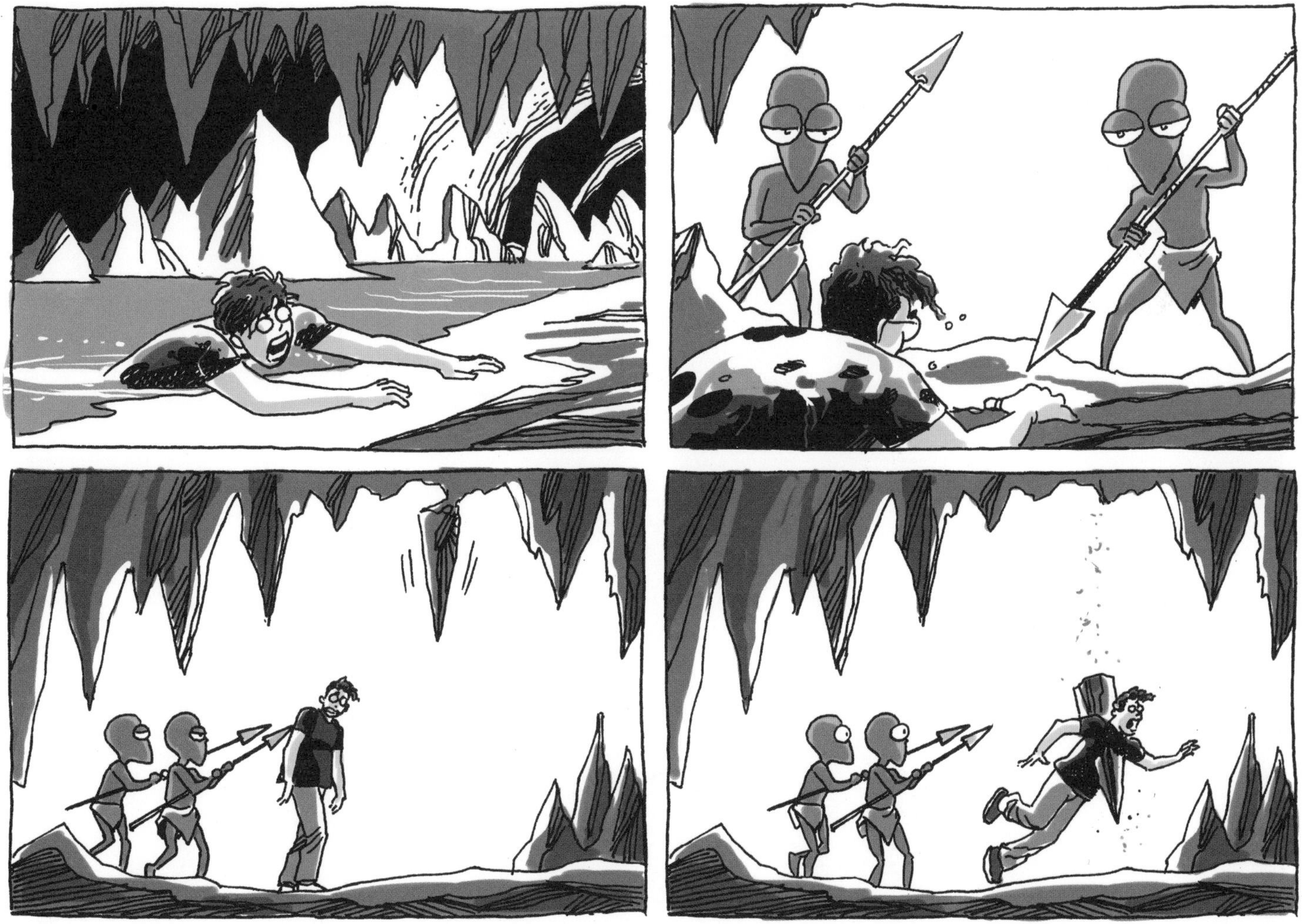

DRIP DROP

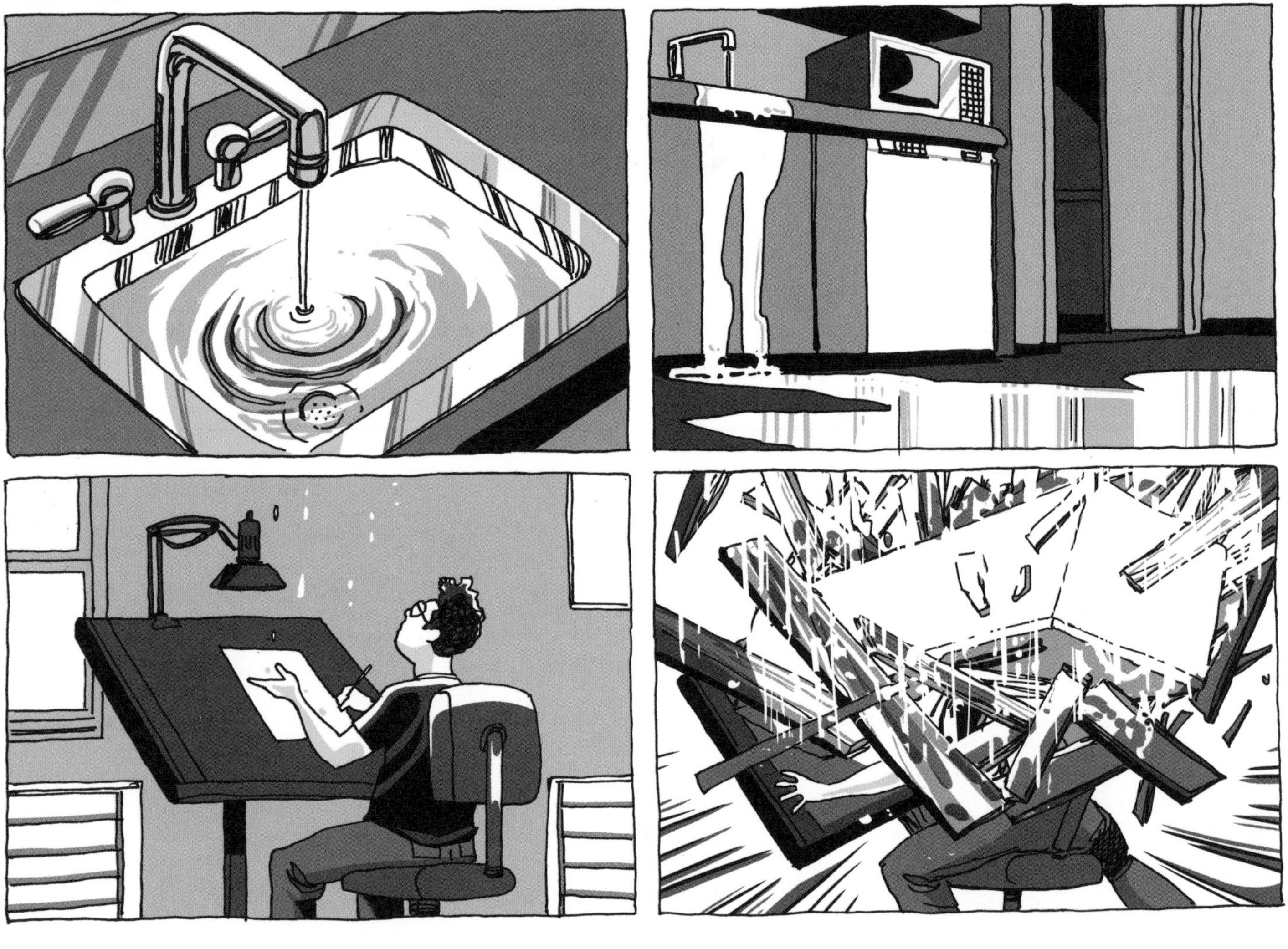

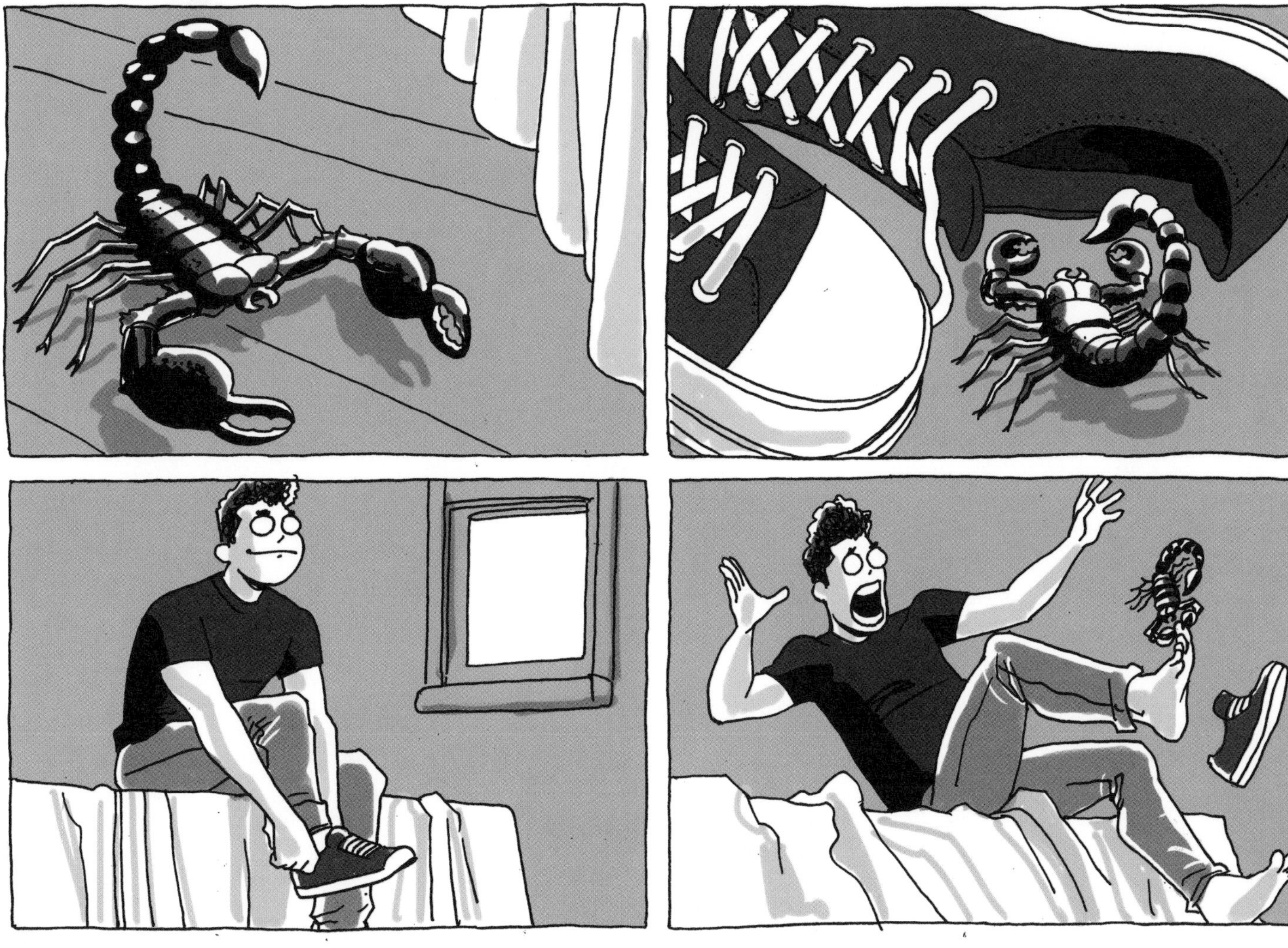

PASTRAMI ON WHEAT

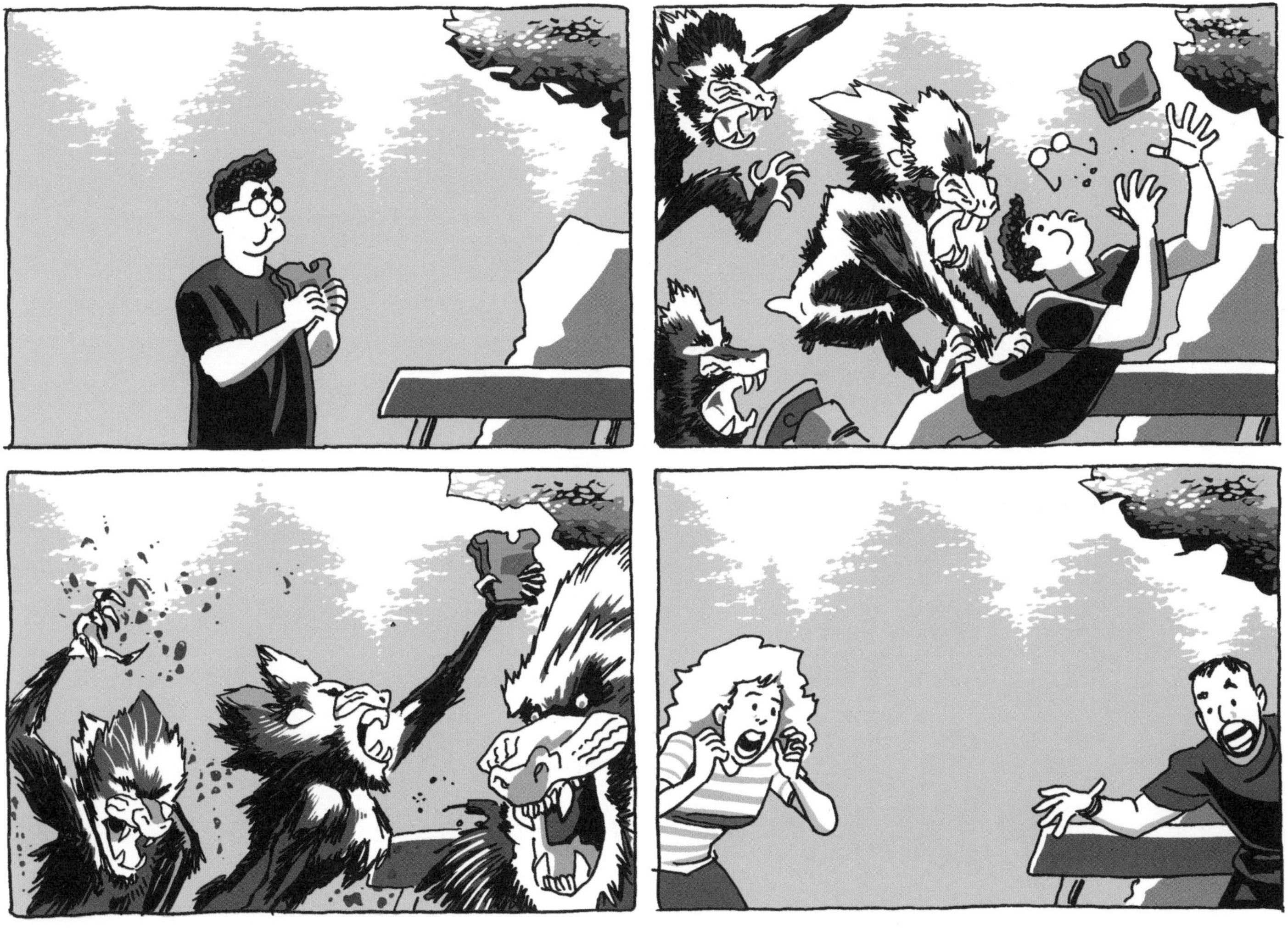

THE MAGIC OF FLIGHT

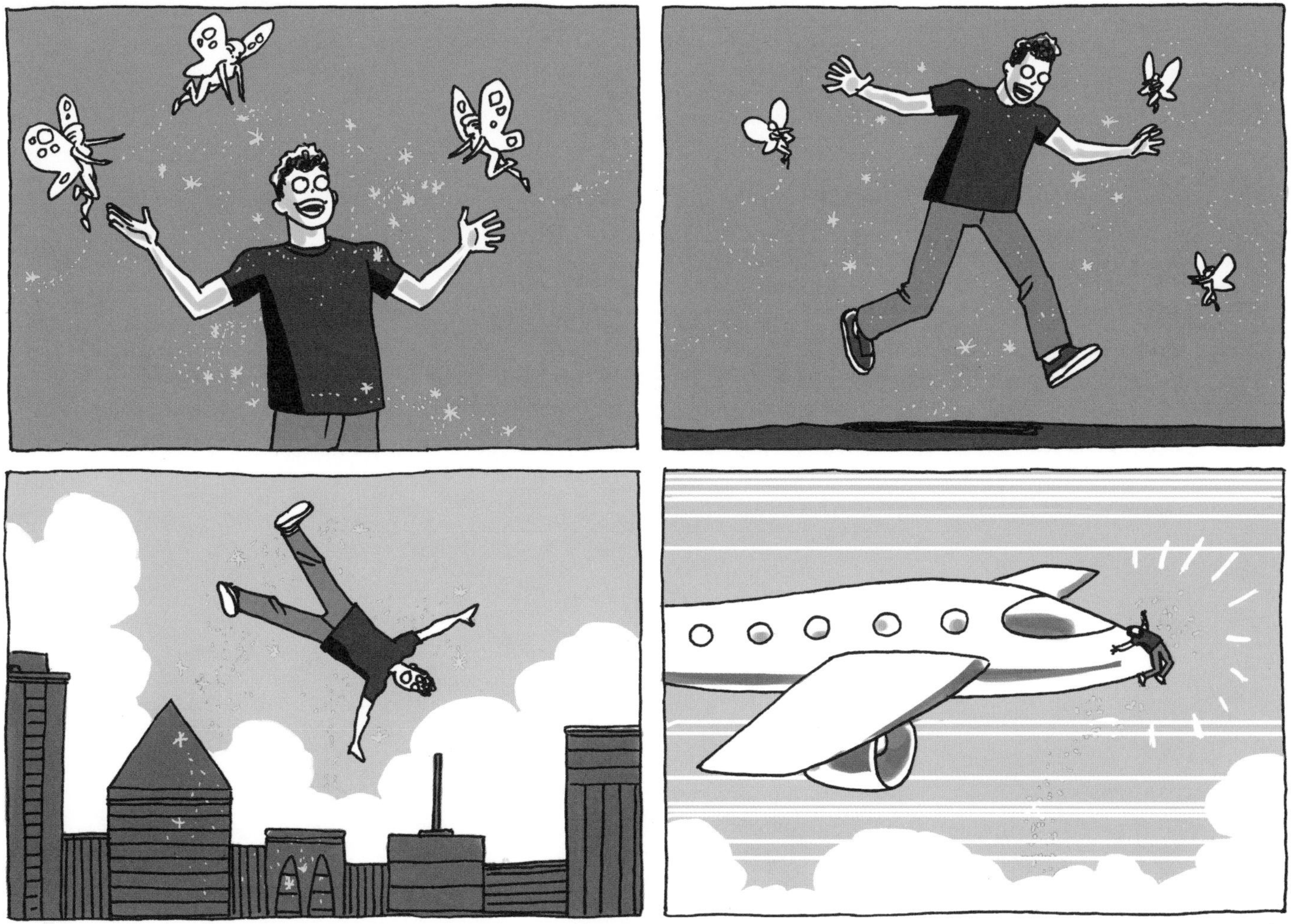

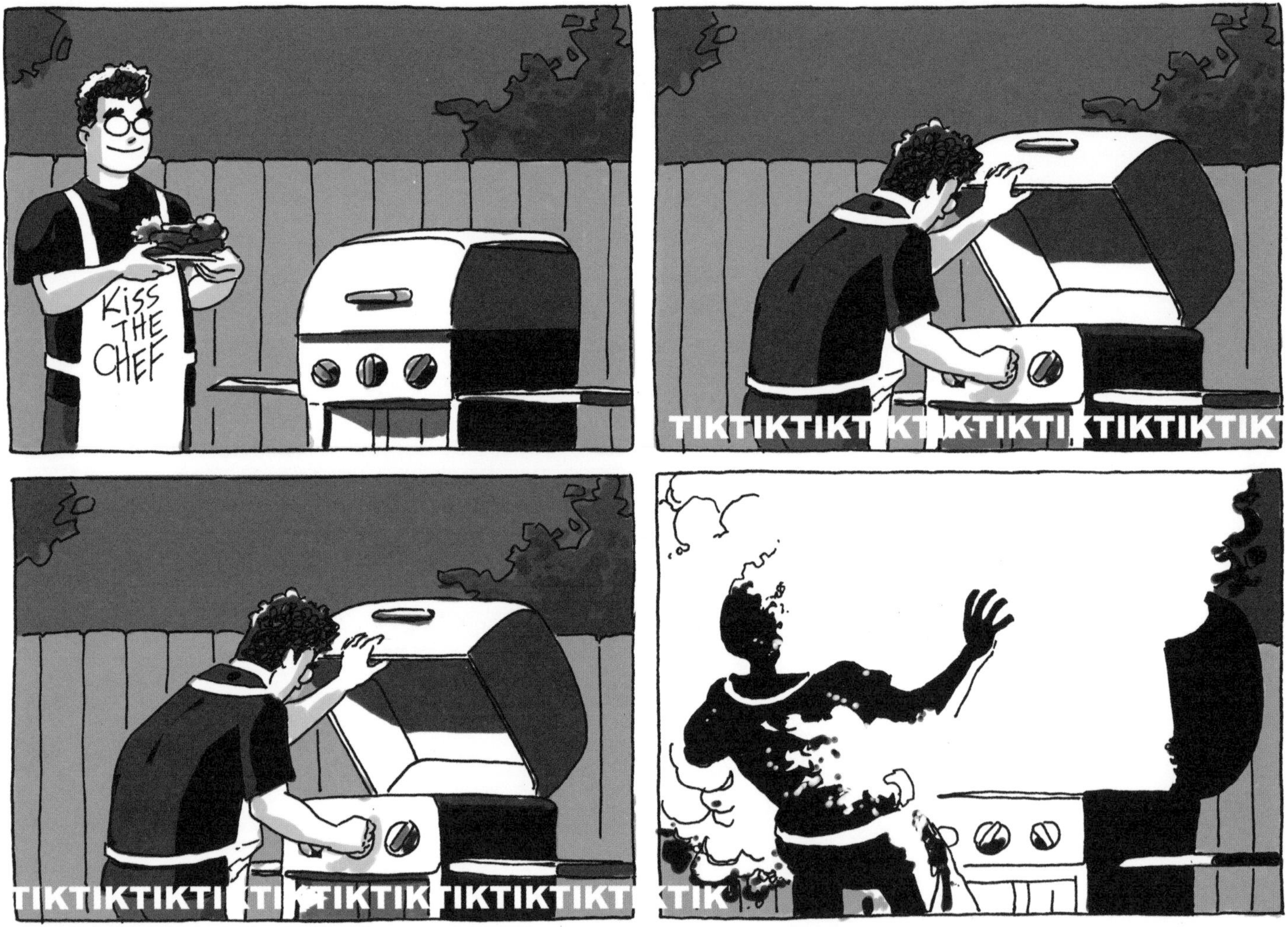
KISS THE CHEF
TIKTIKTIKT KT KTIKTI KTIKTIKTIKT
TIKTIKTIKTI KTI TIKTIK TIKTIKTIKT KTIK

WATER, WATER, EVERYWHERE

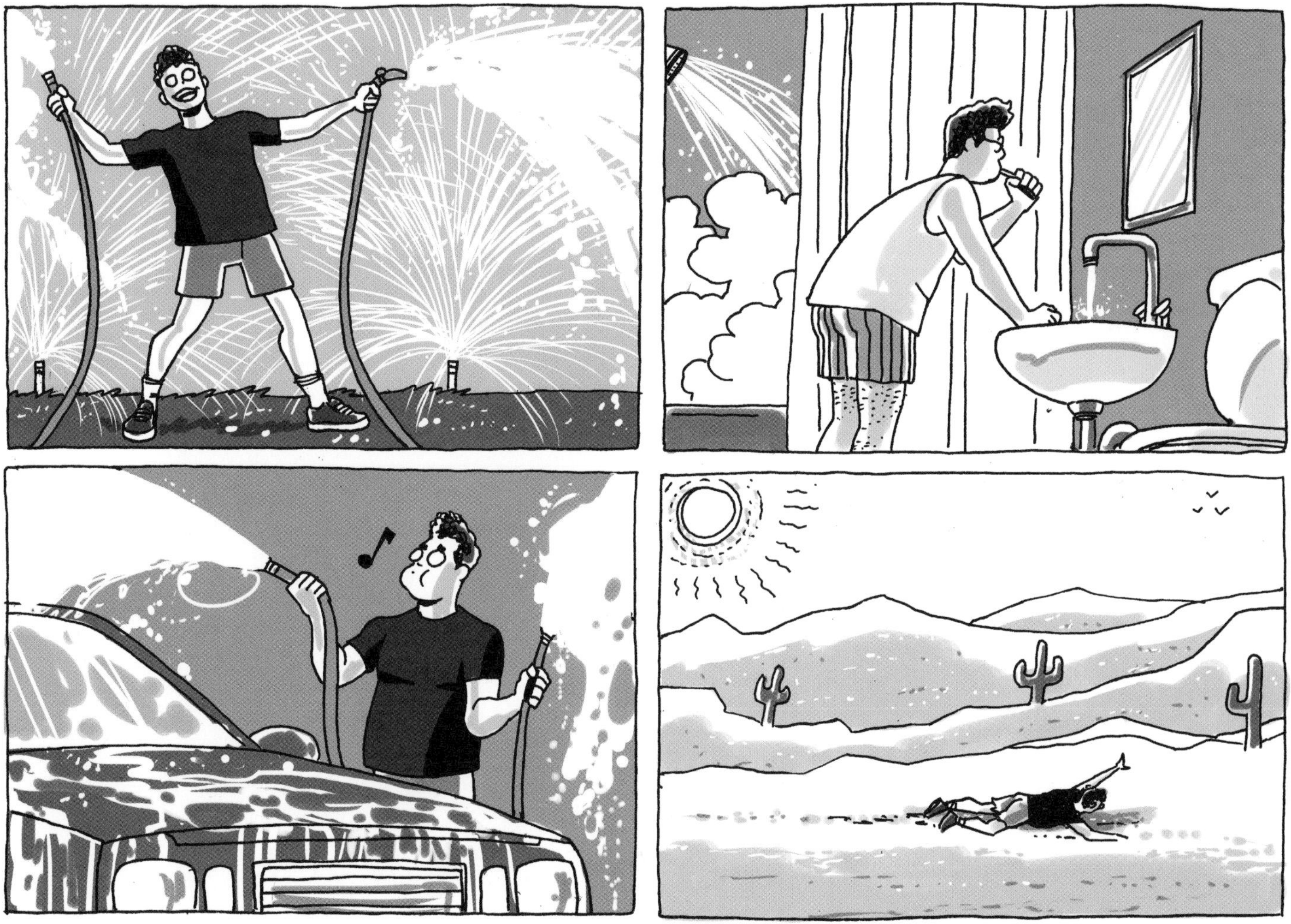

NOTHING TO SEE HERE

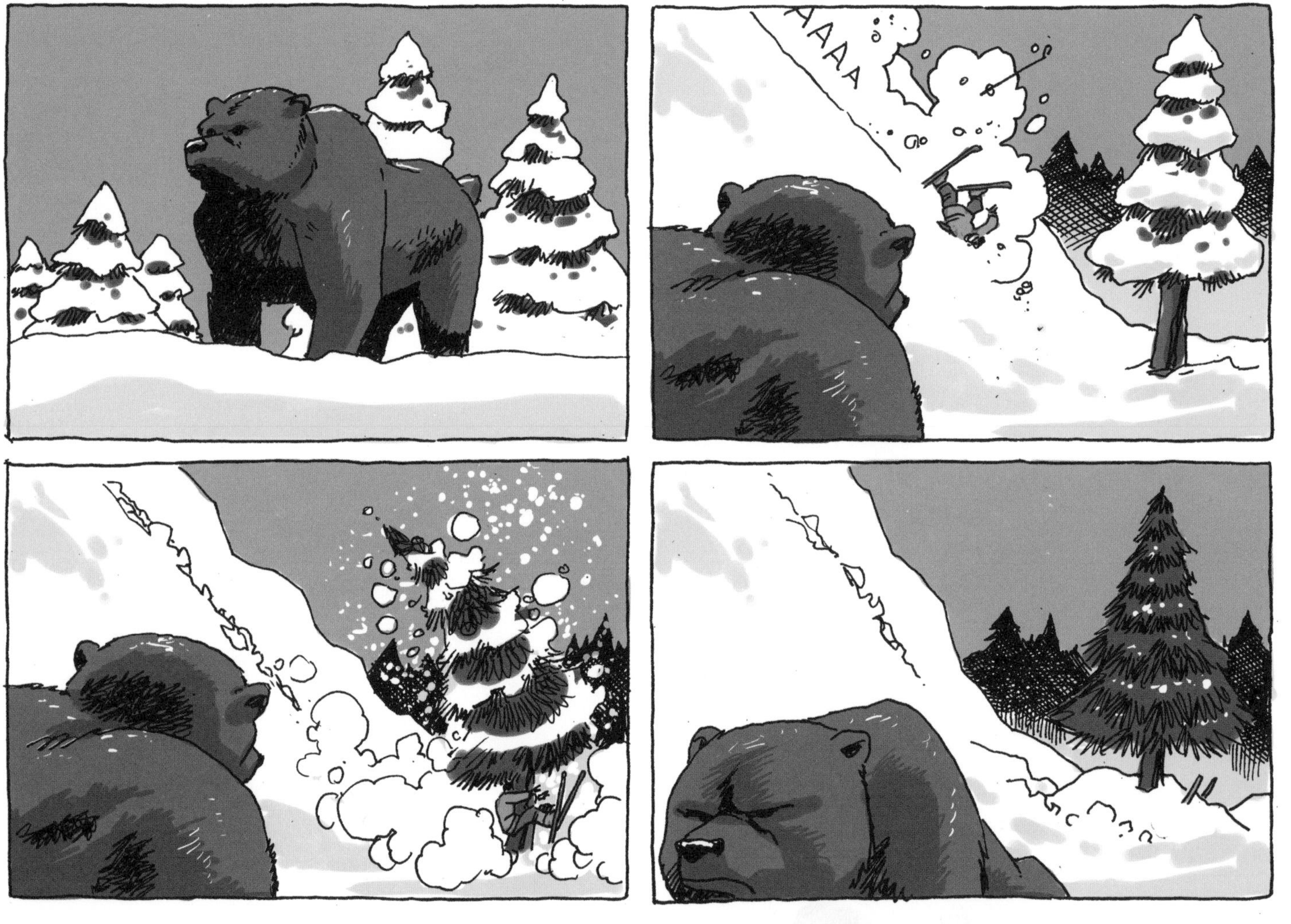
AAAA

A VISITOR

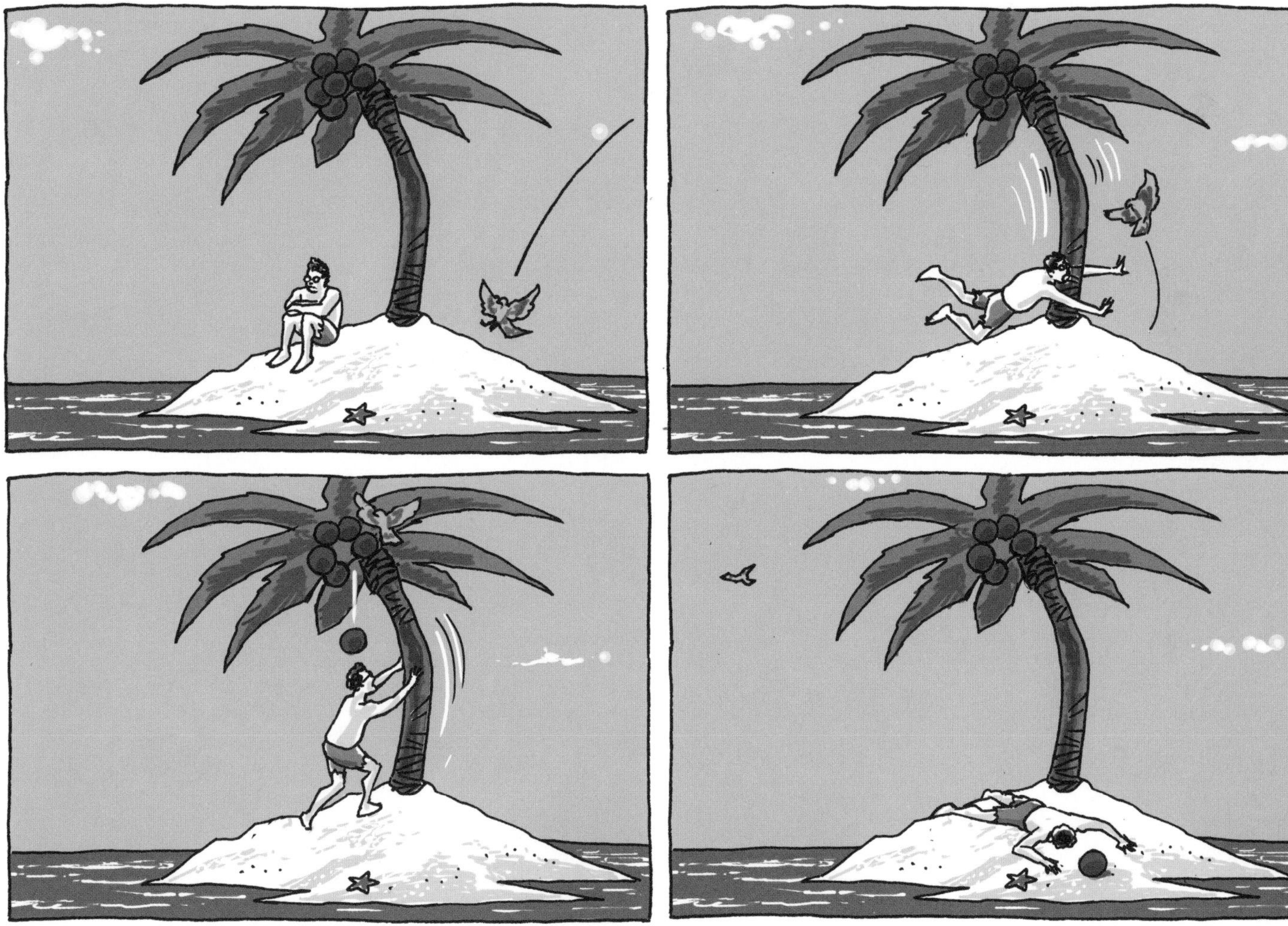

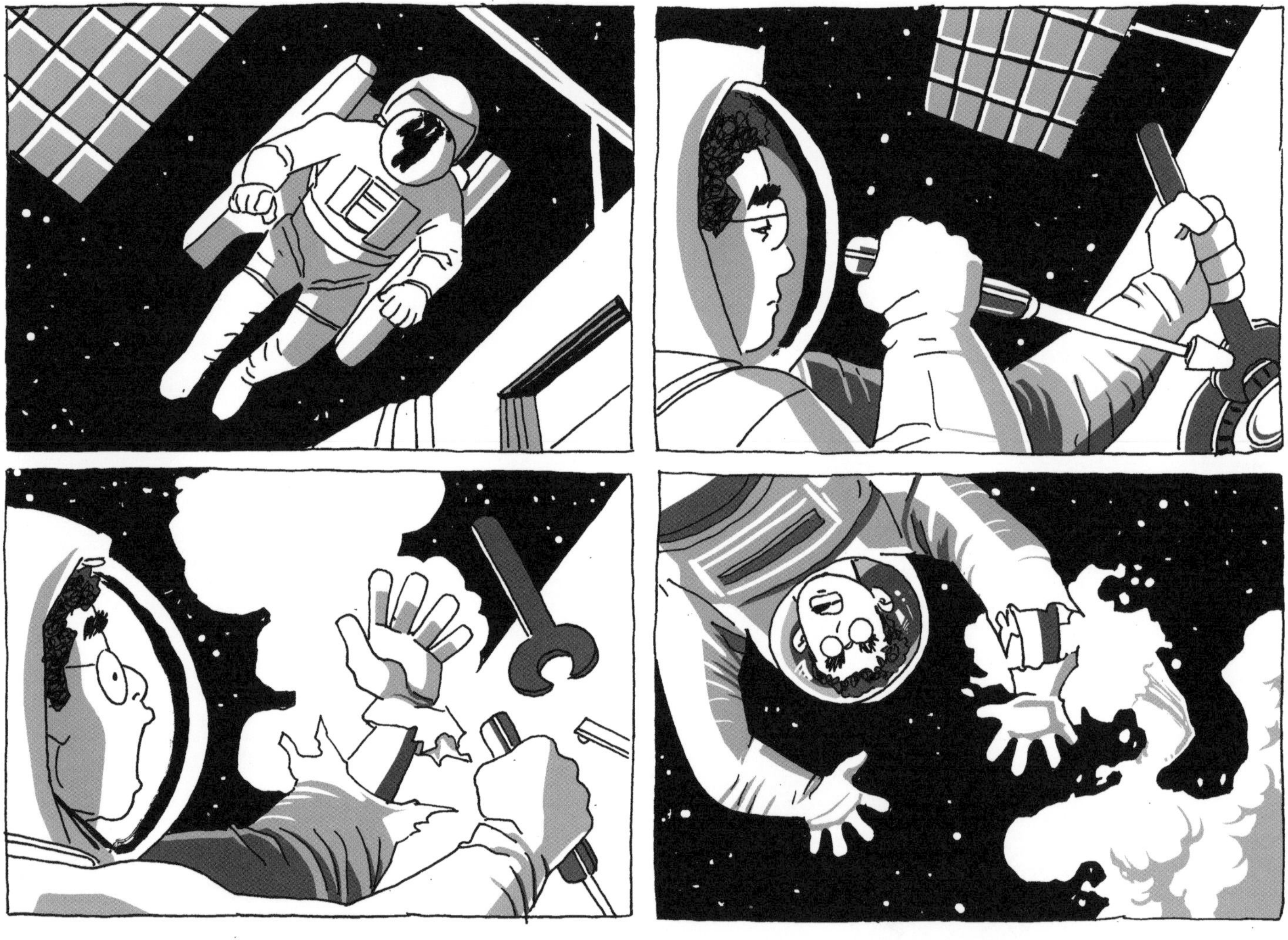

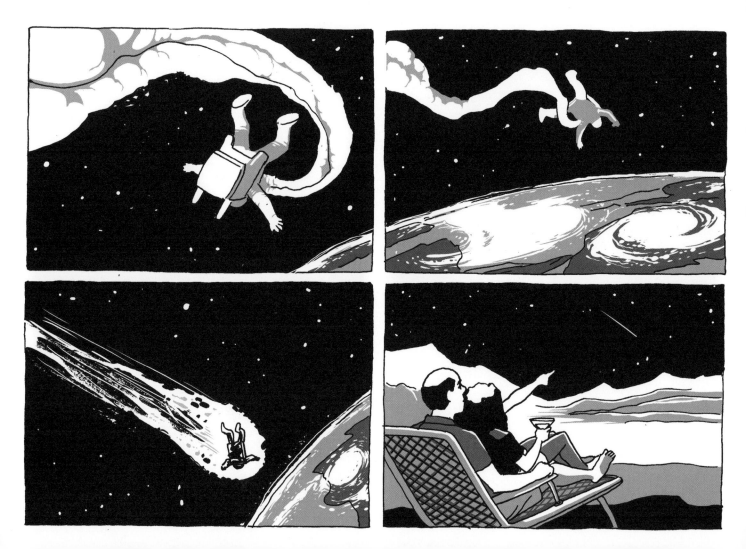

DO YOU EVEN LIFT, BRO?

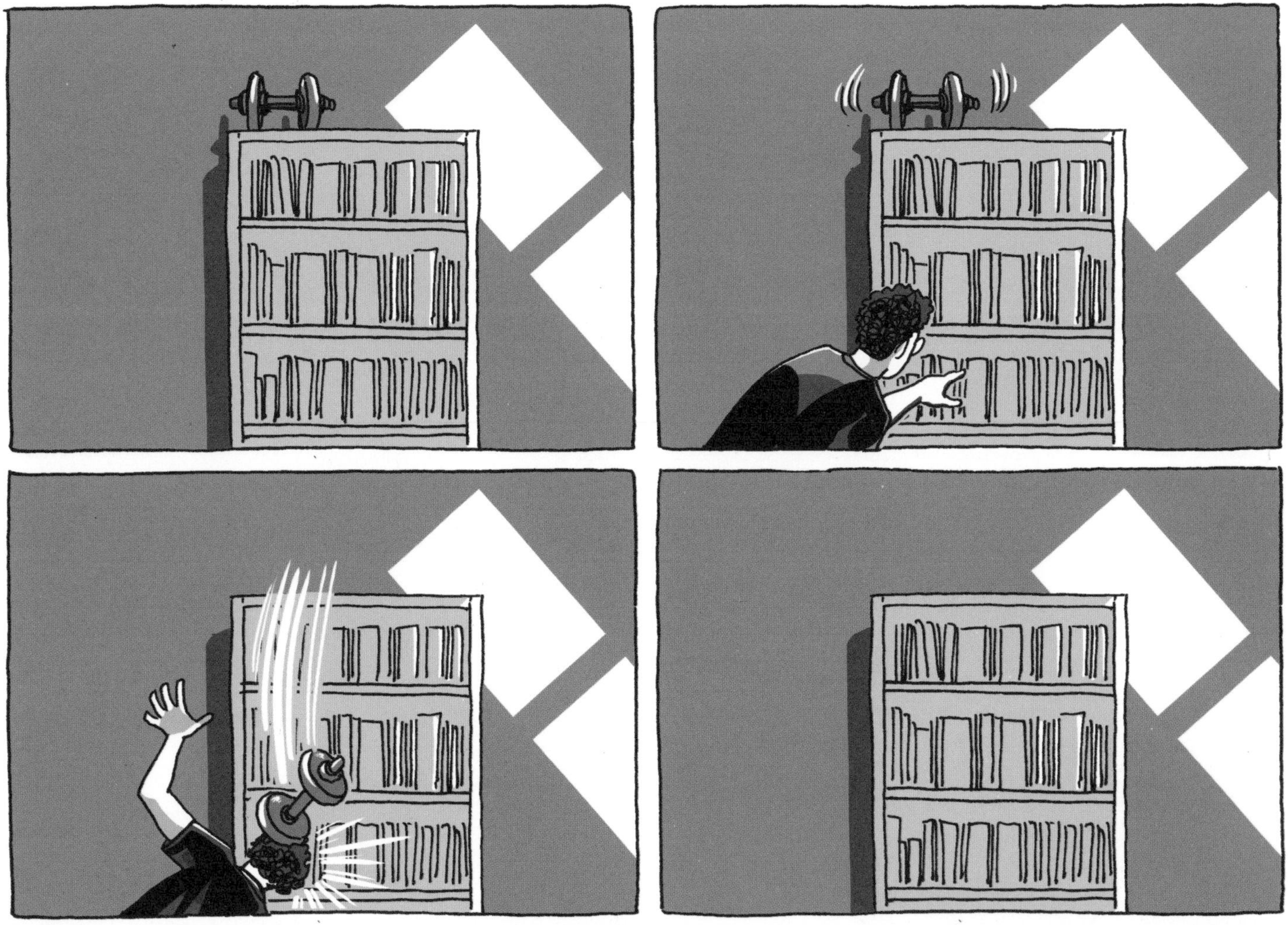

THE MOST IMPORTANT MEAL OF THE DAY

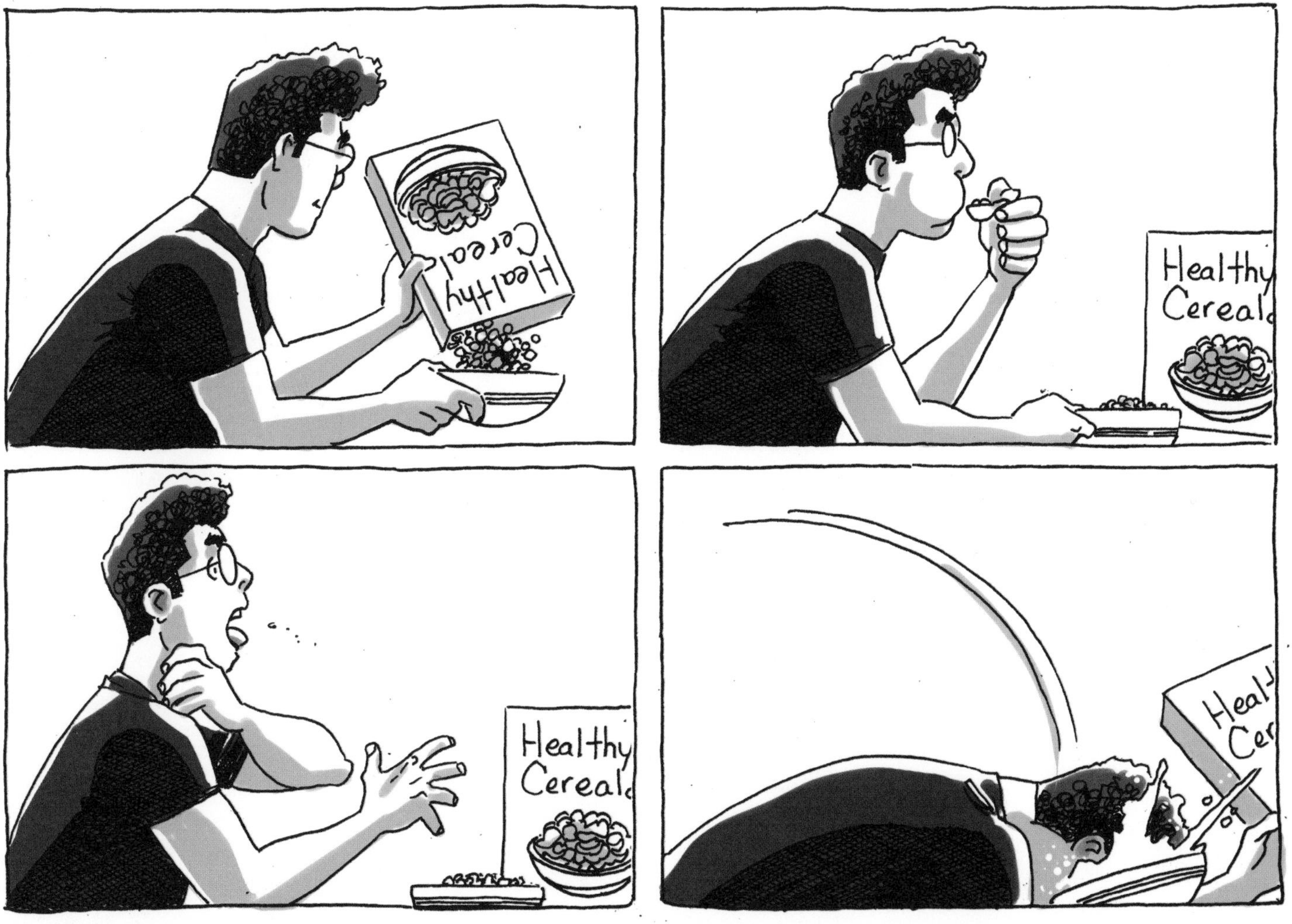
Healthy Cereal
Healthy Cereal
Healthy Cereal

NAPTIME

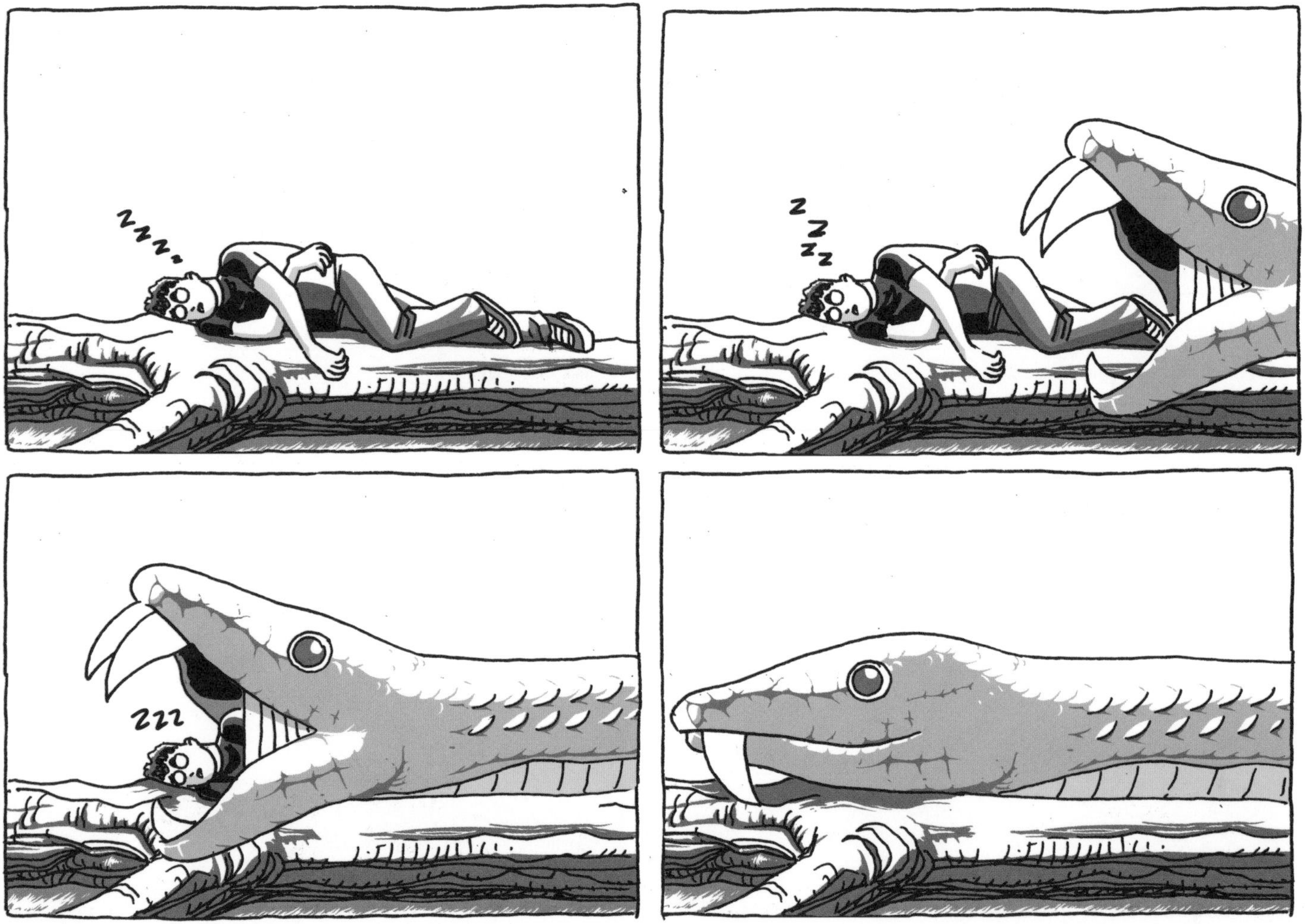
ZZZZ
ZZZZ
ZZZ

ECHOOOO!

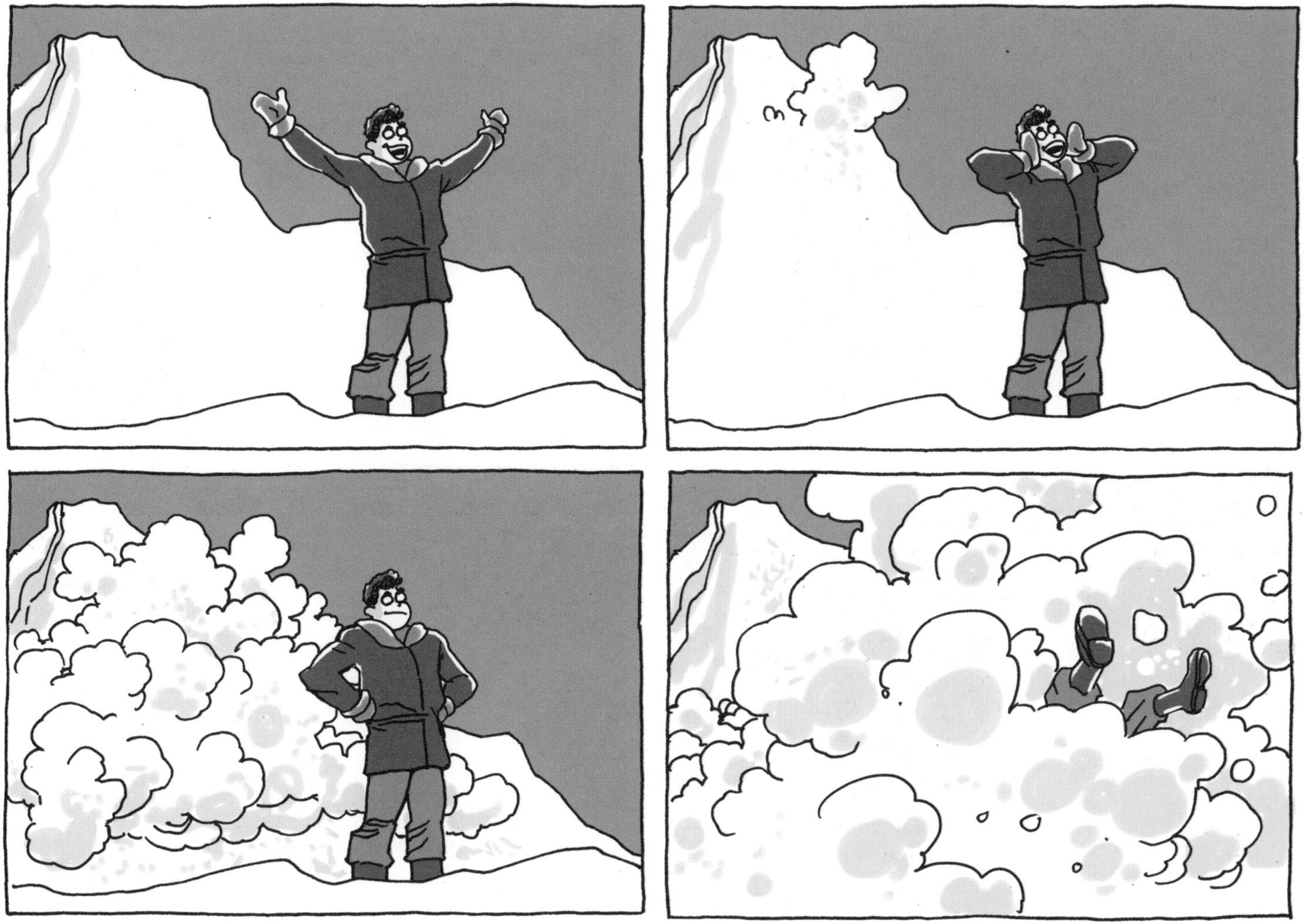

FIRST CONTACT

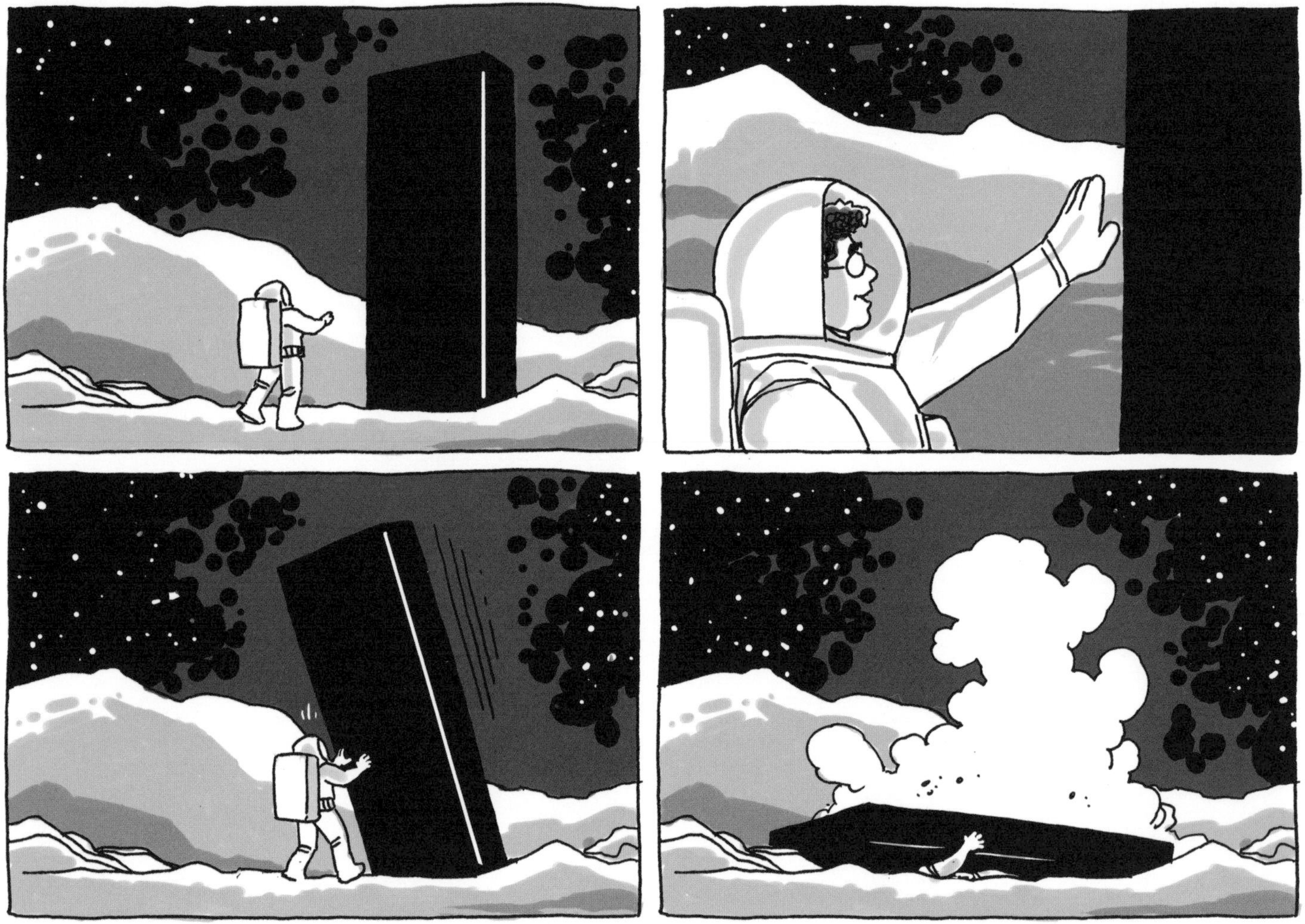

ROAD WORK

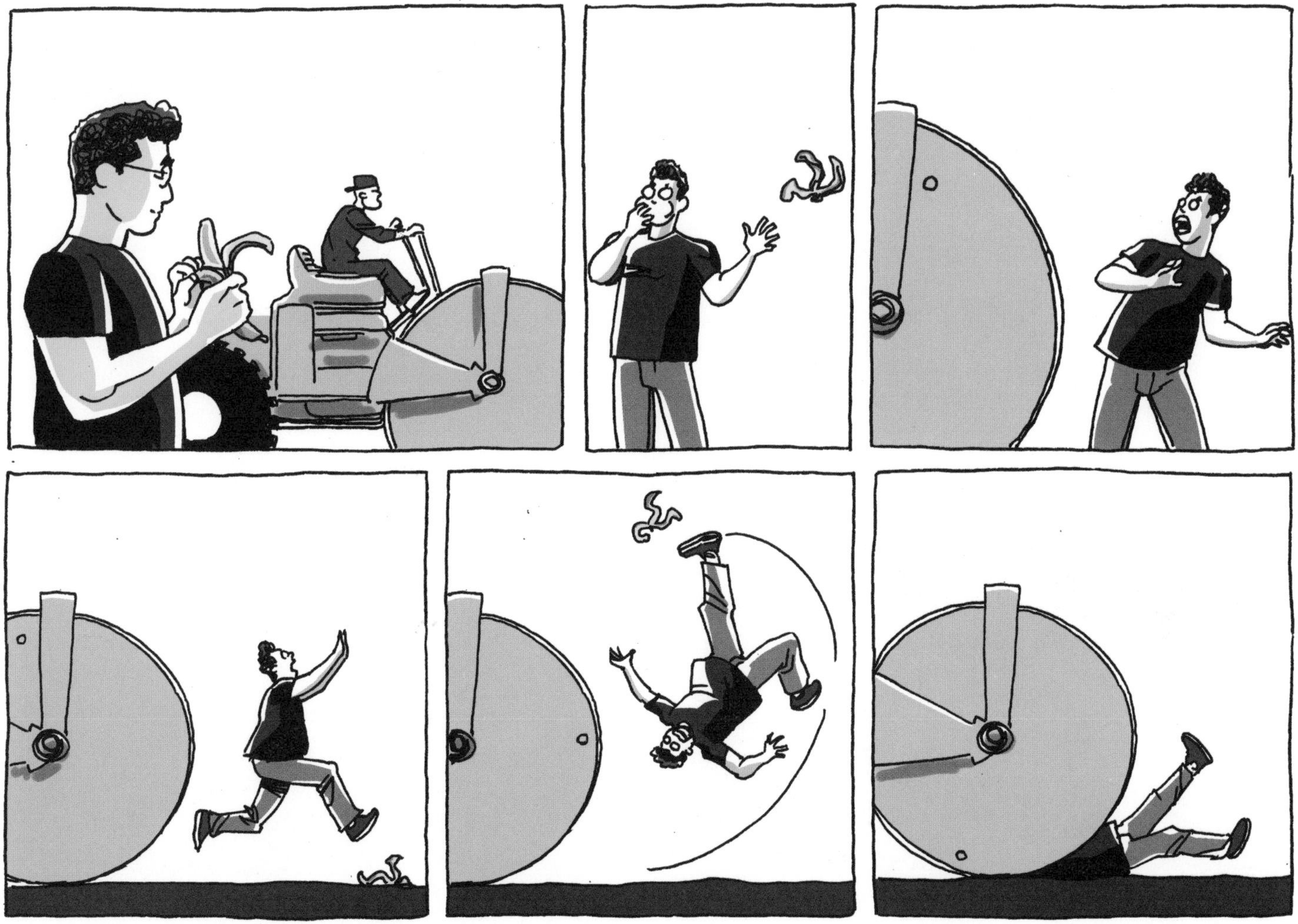

O CHRISTMAS TREE

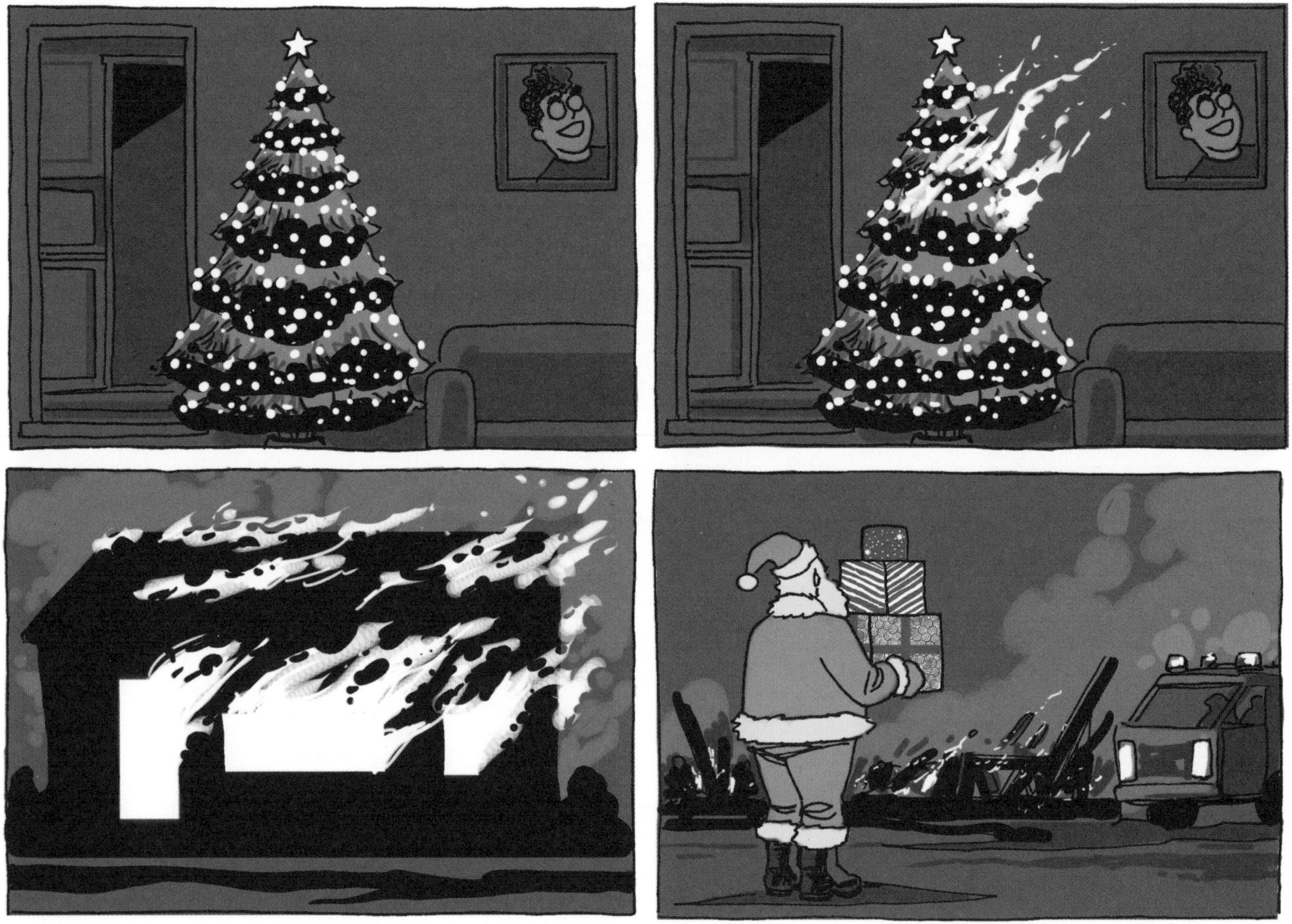

KIBBLE

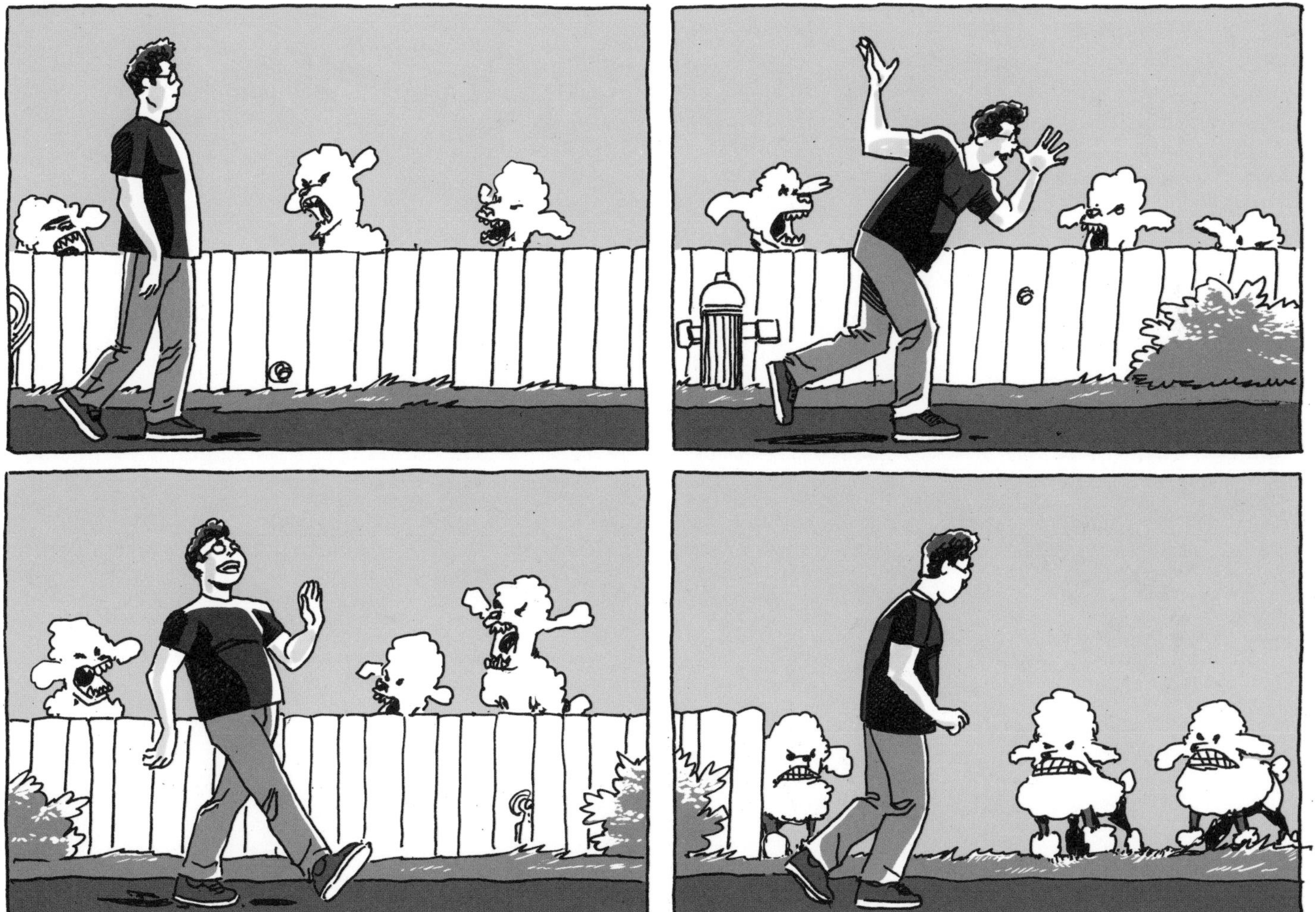

RED DELICIOUS

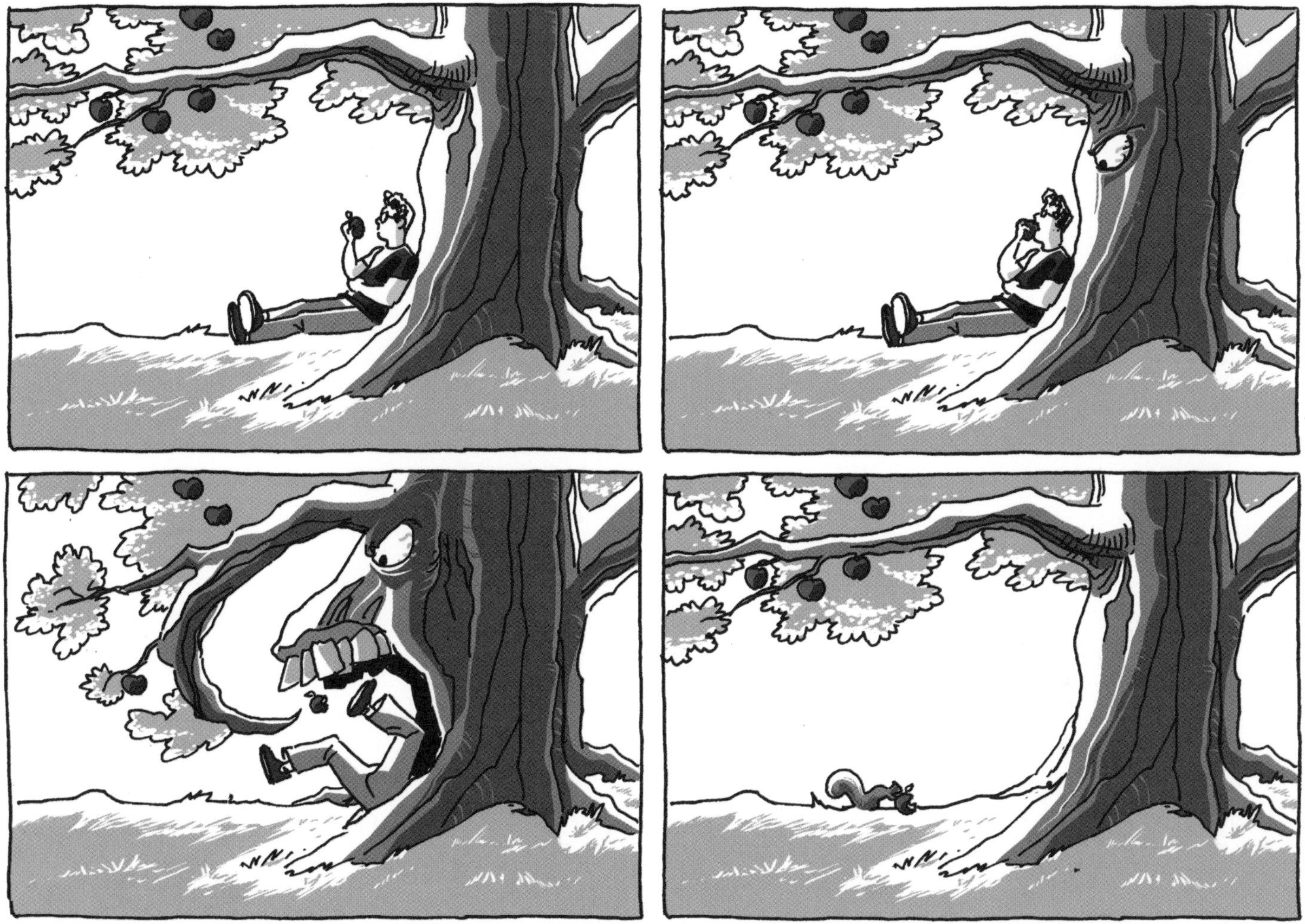

THE FOURTH KIND

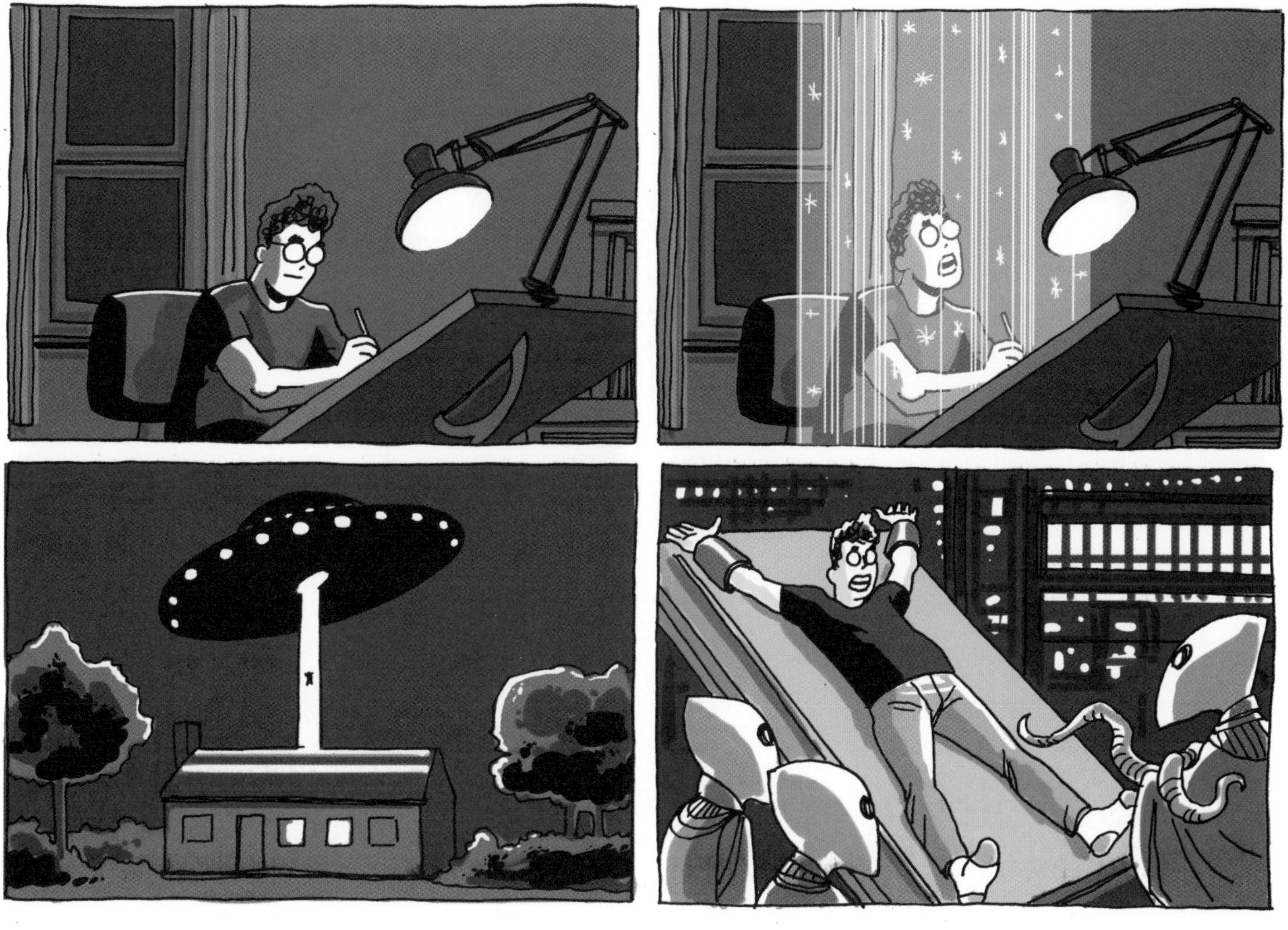

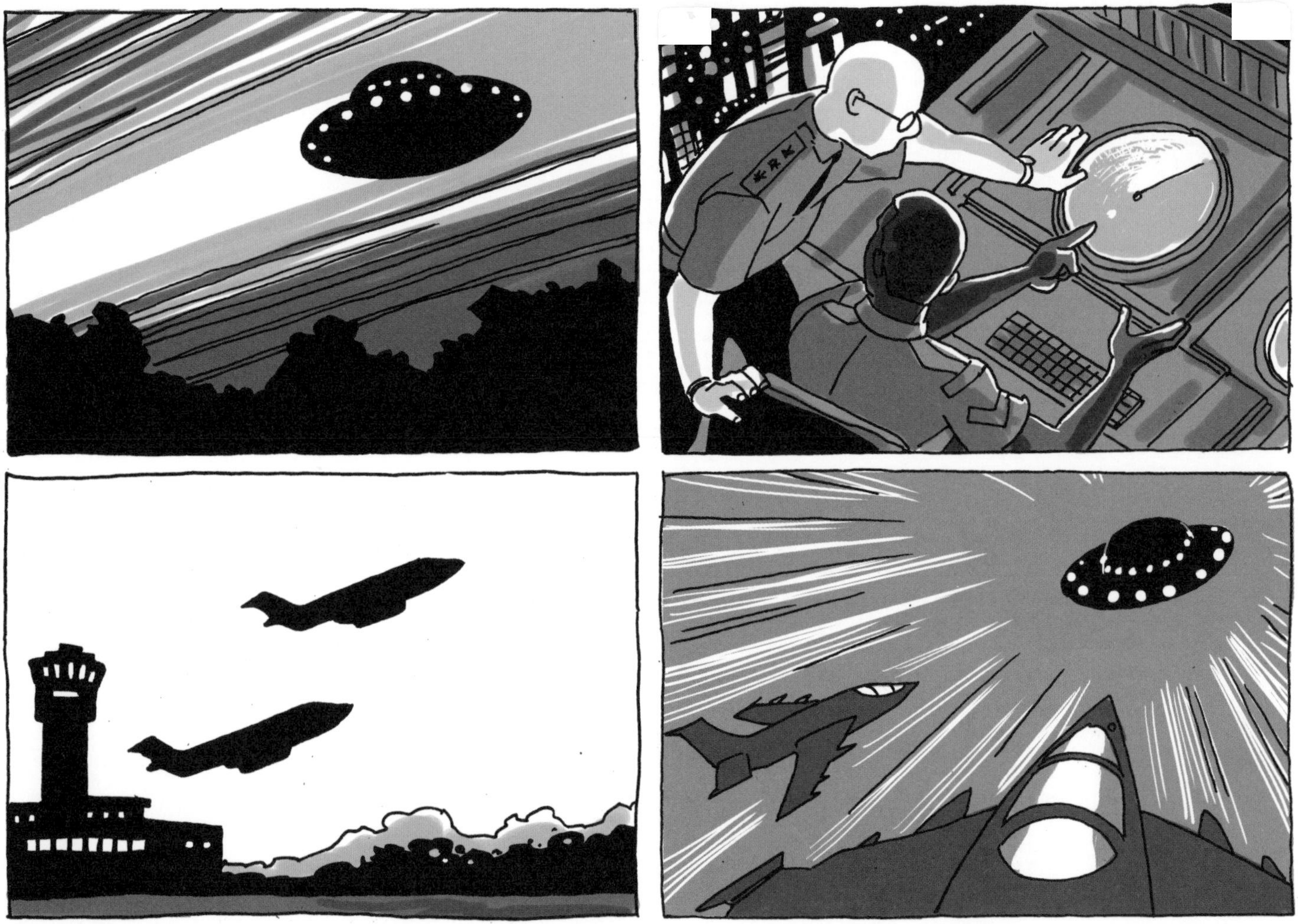

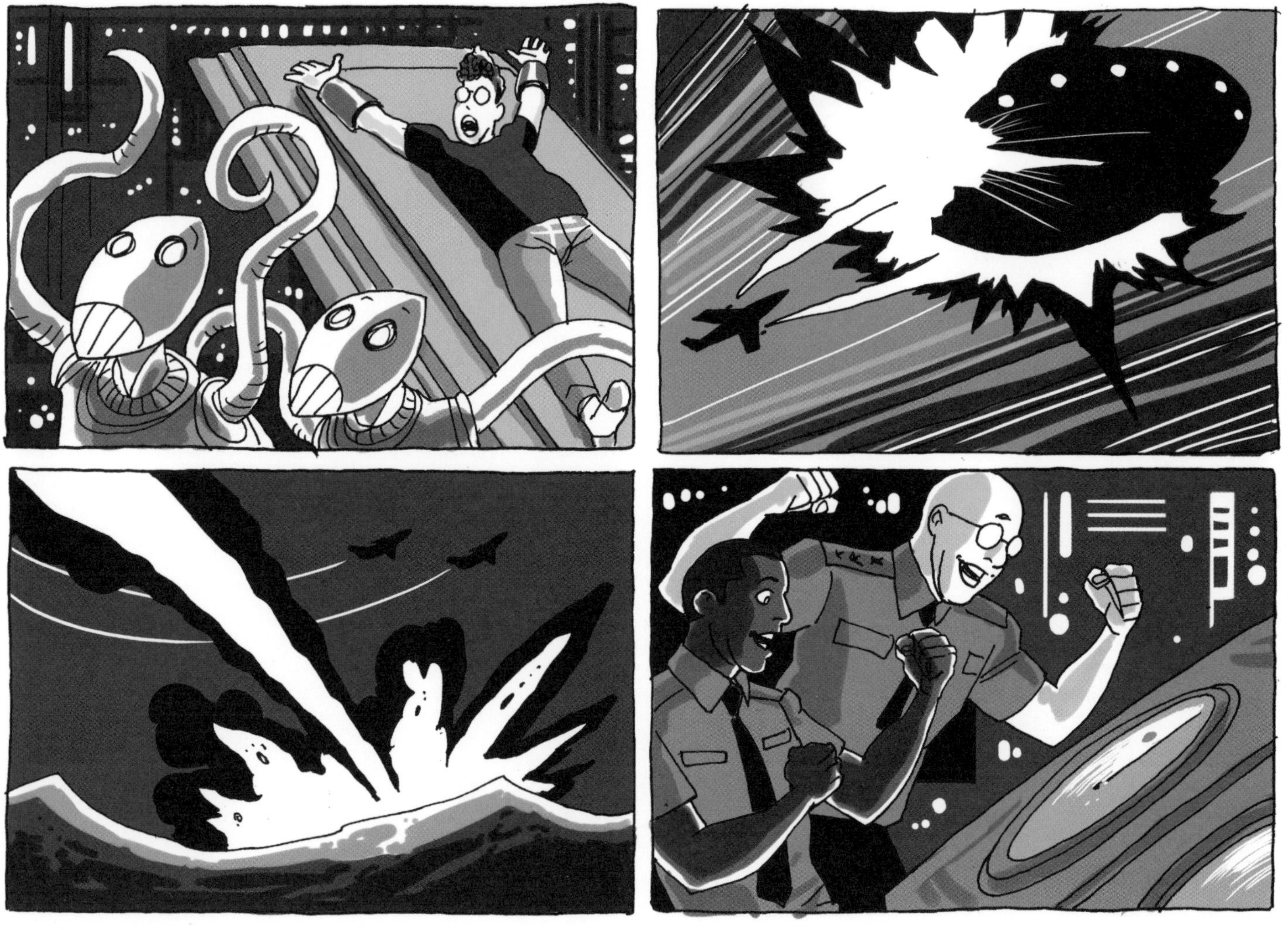

GREEN THUMB

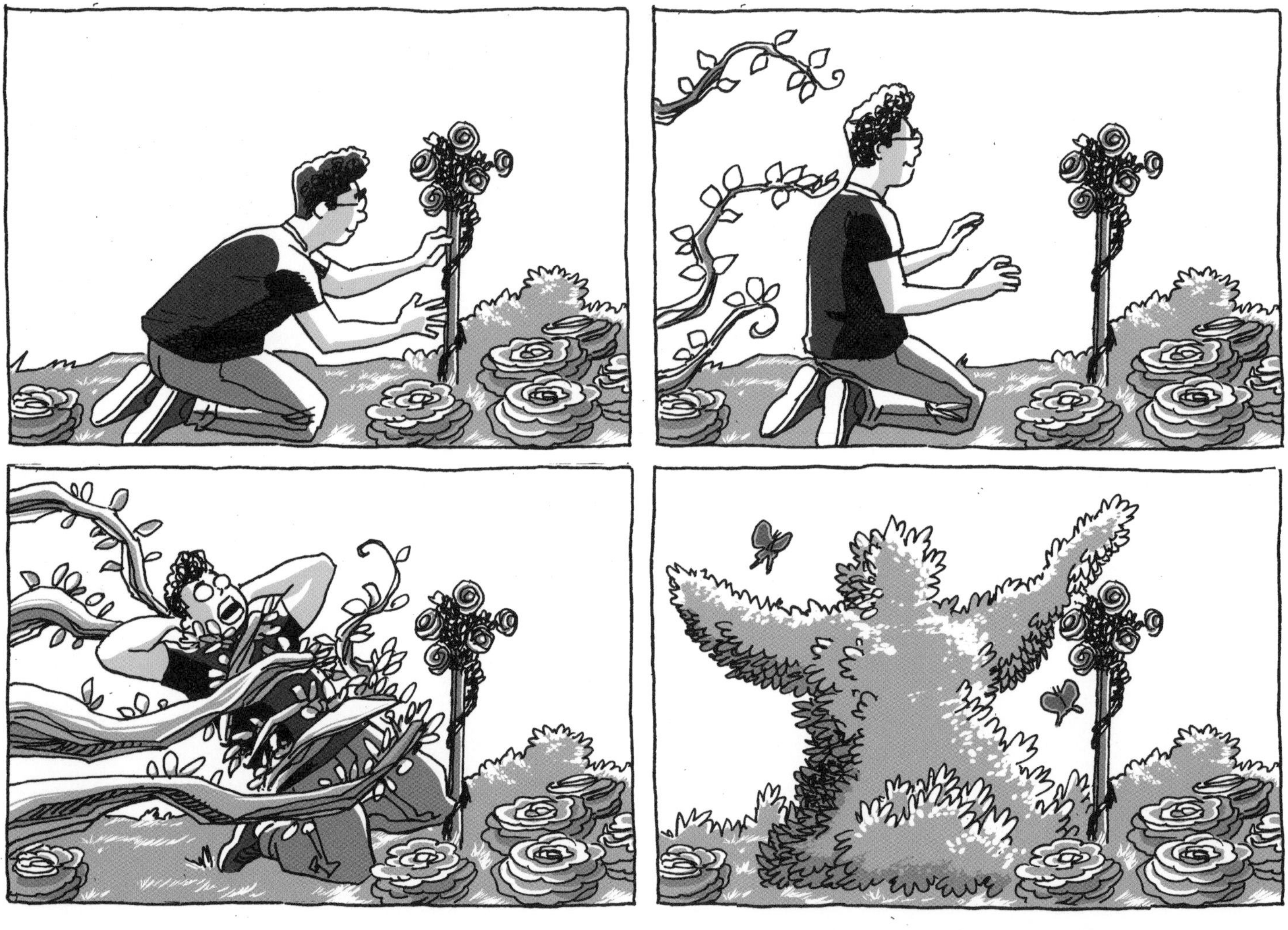

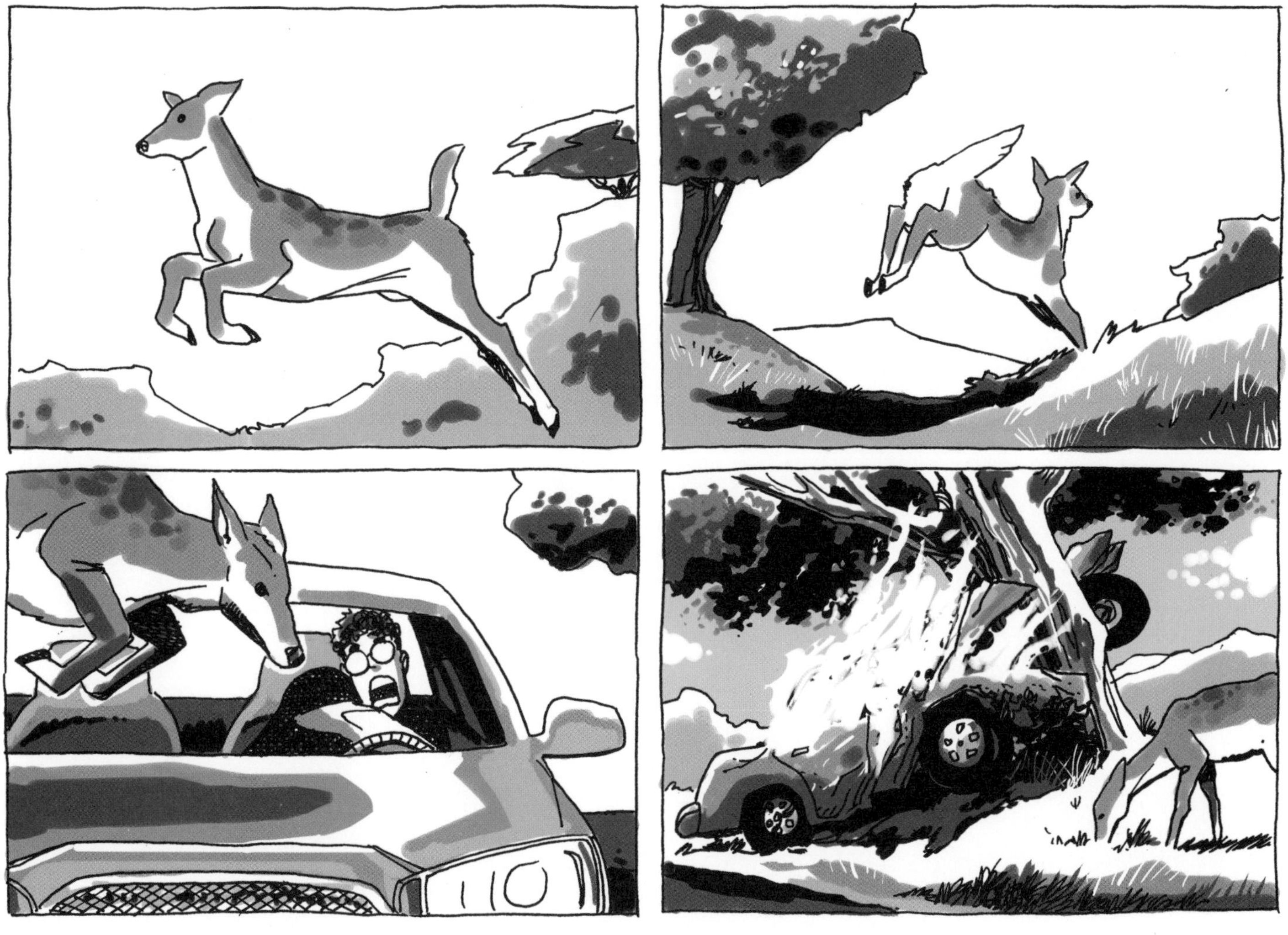

SLEEP TIGHT

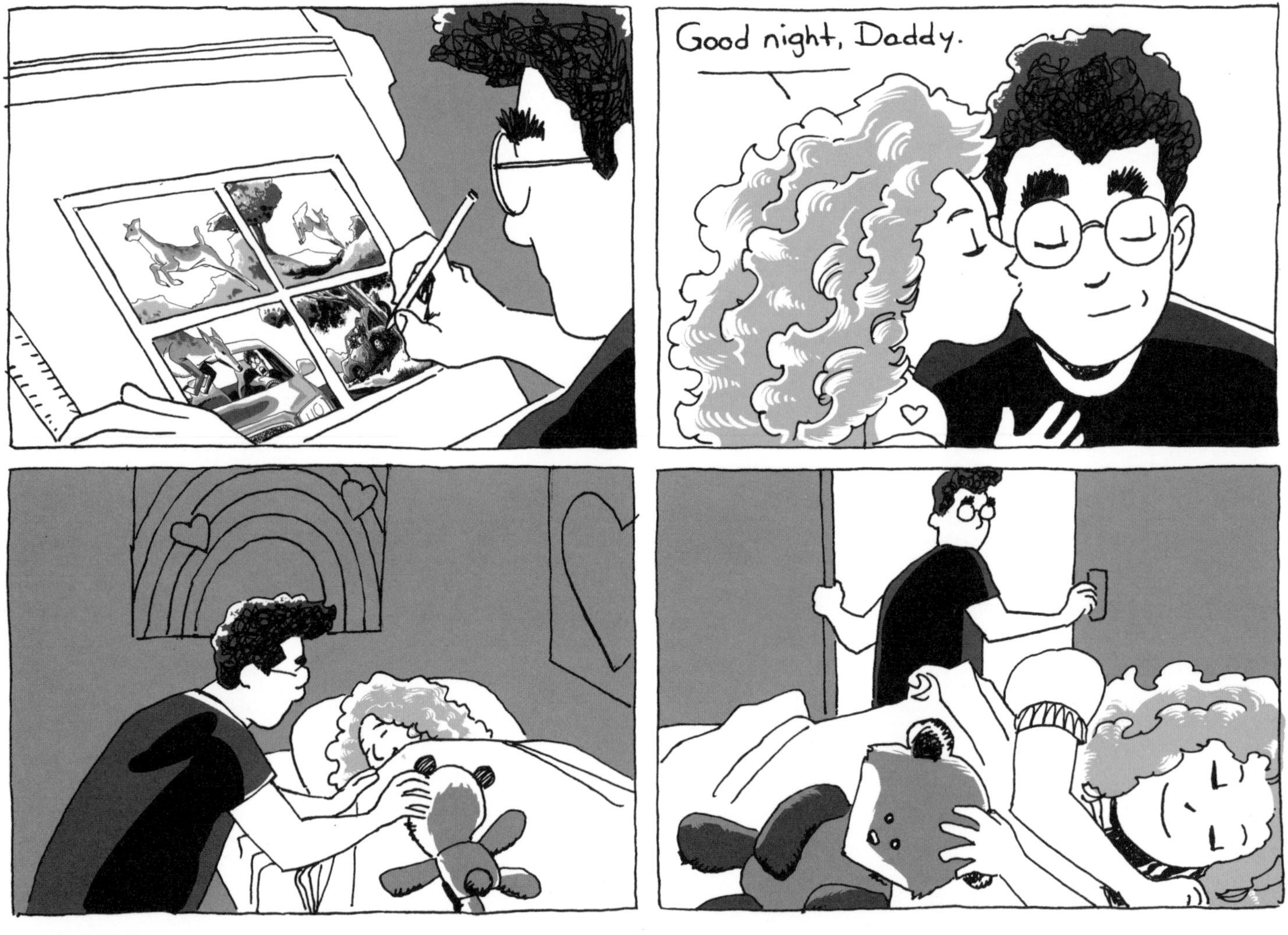
Good night, Daddy.

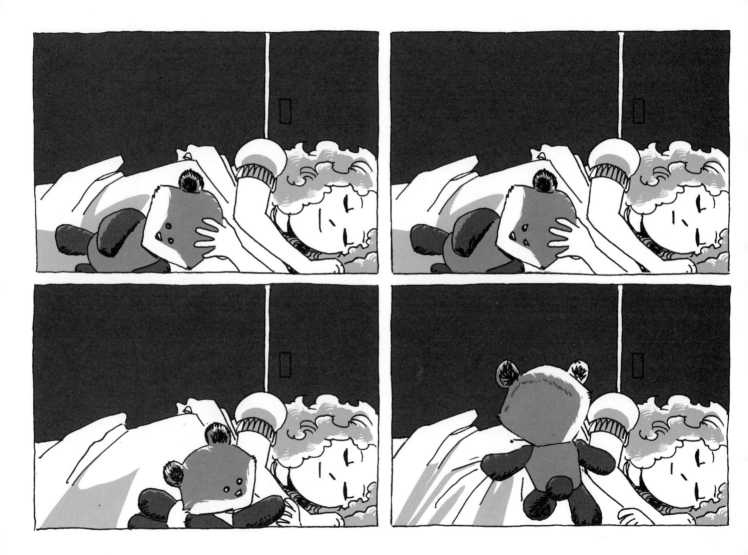

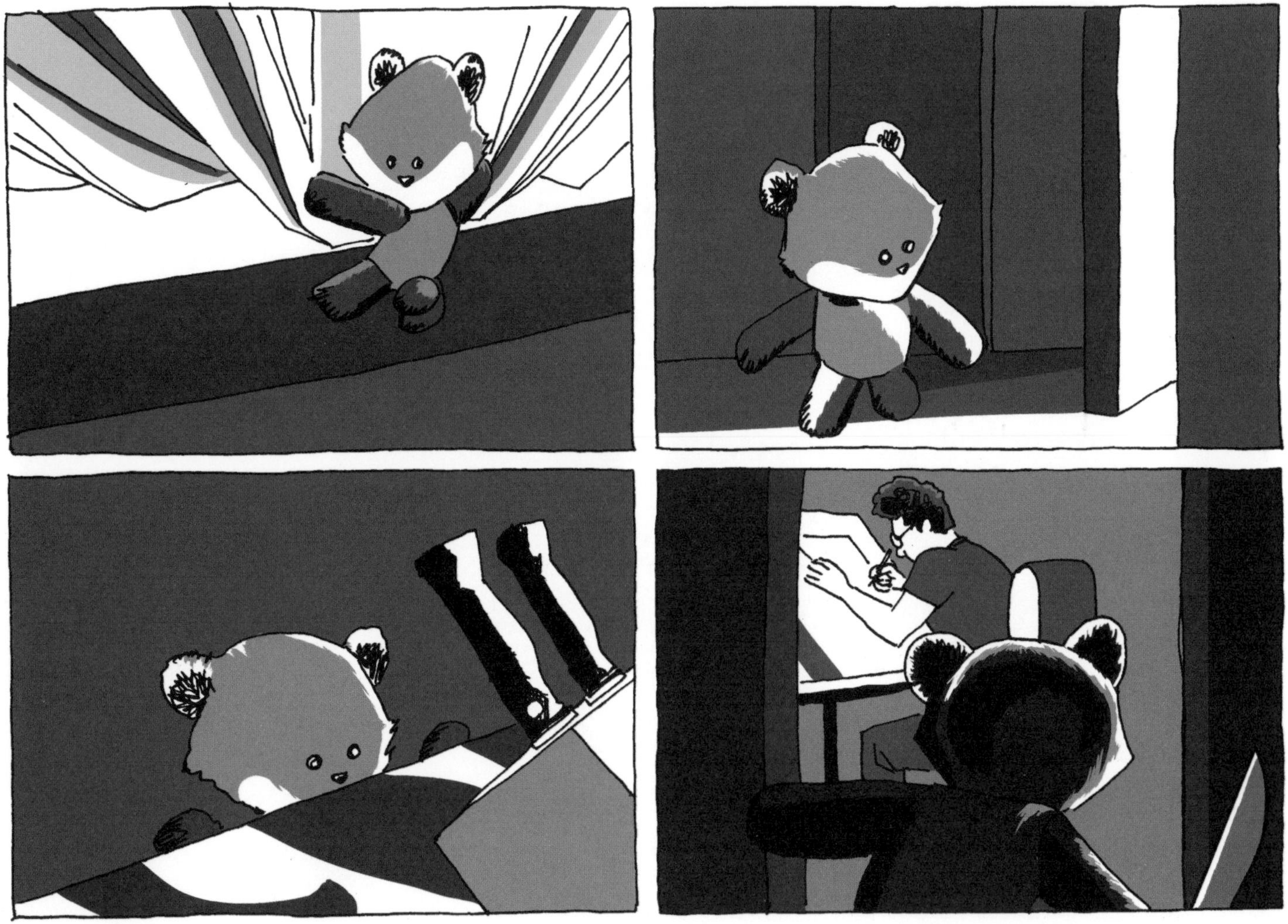

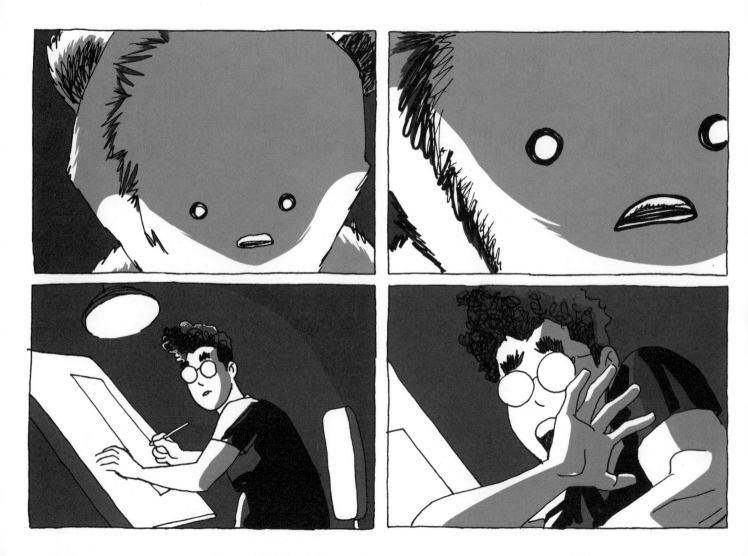

TIMBER

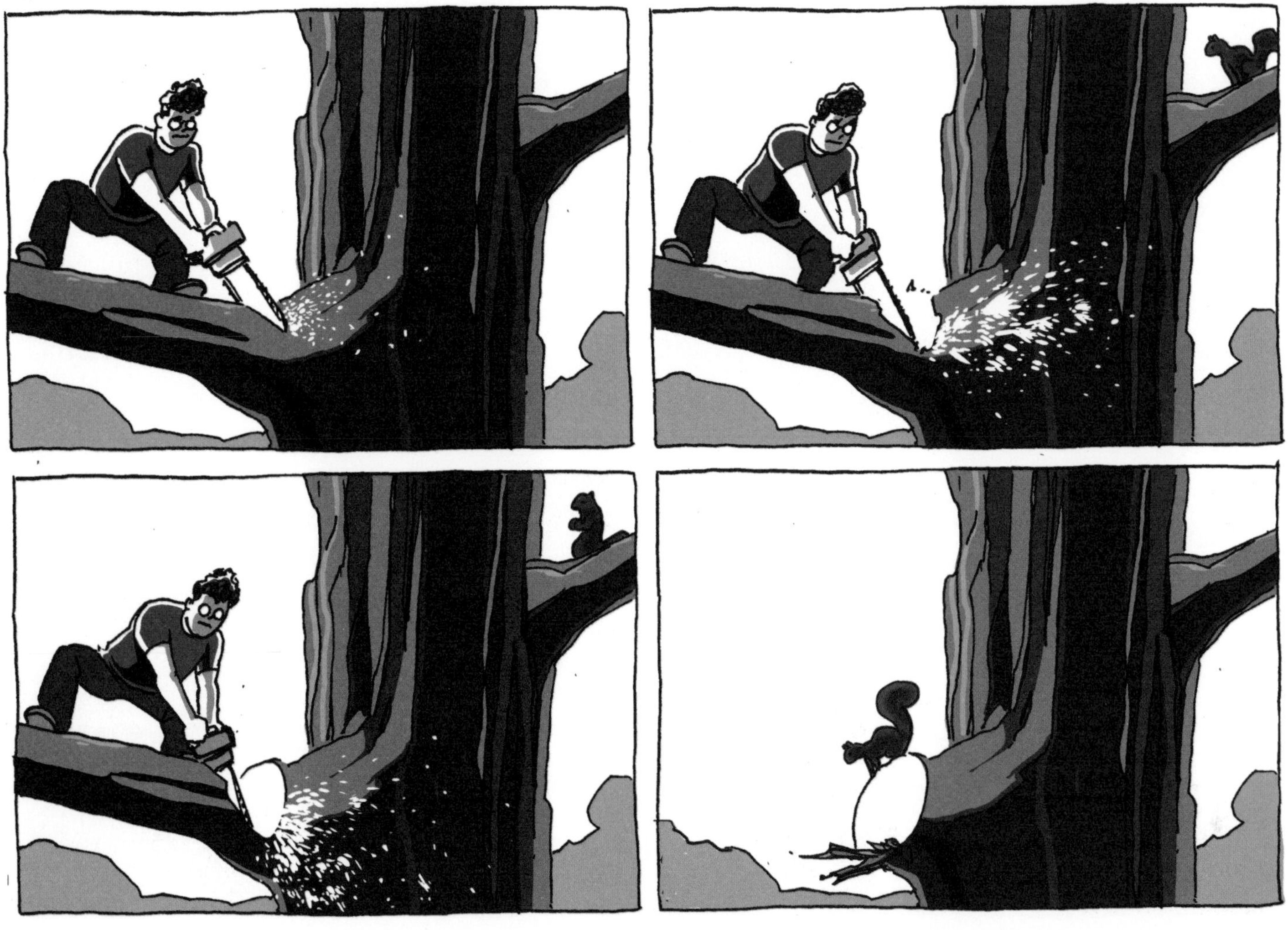

A LITTLE HELP

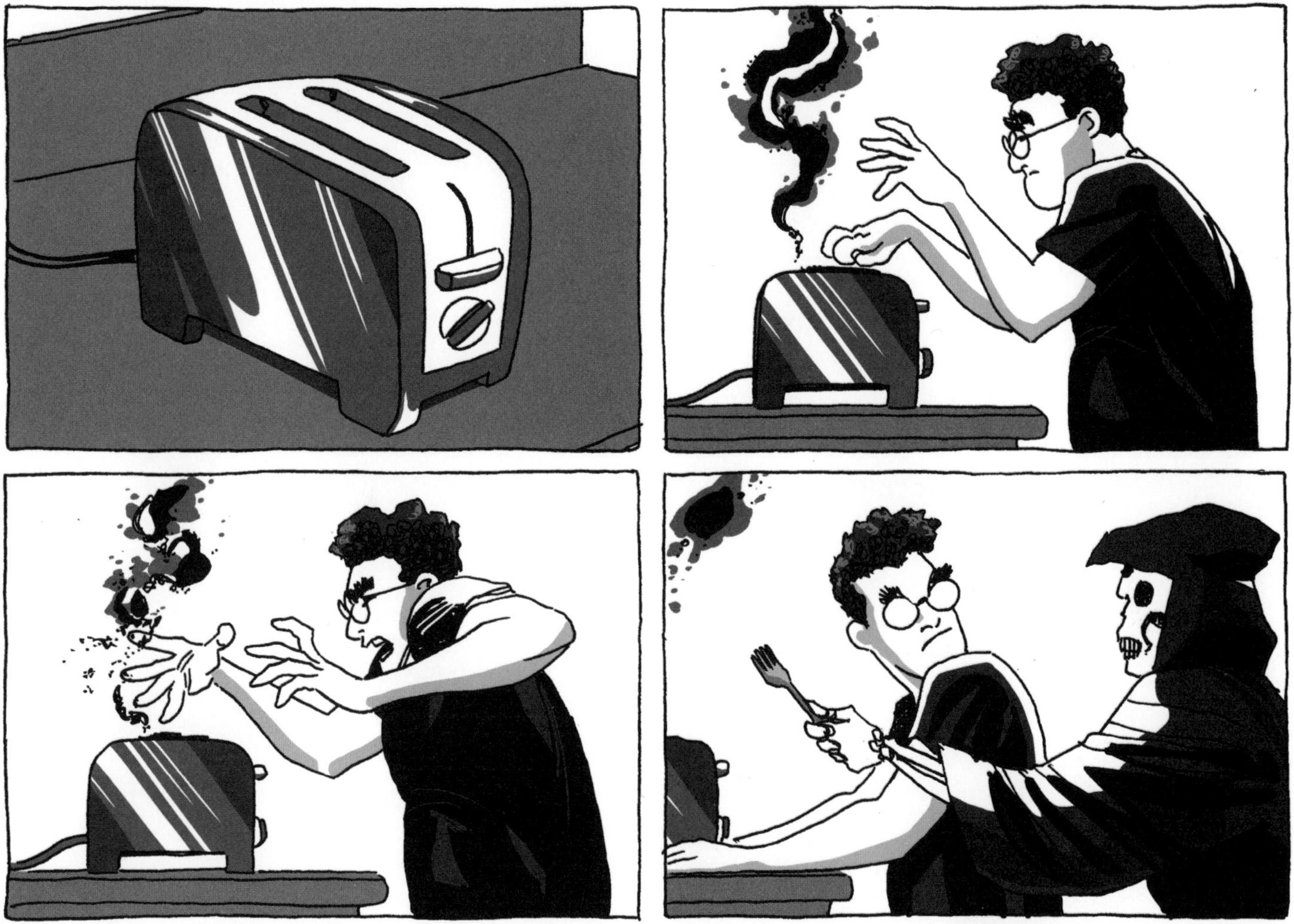

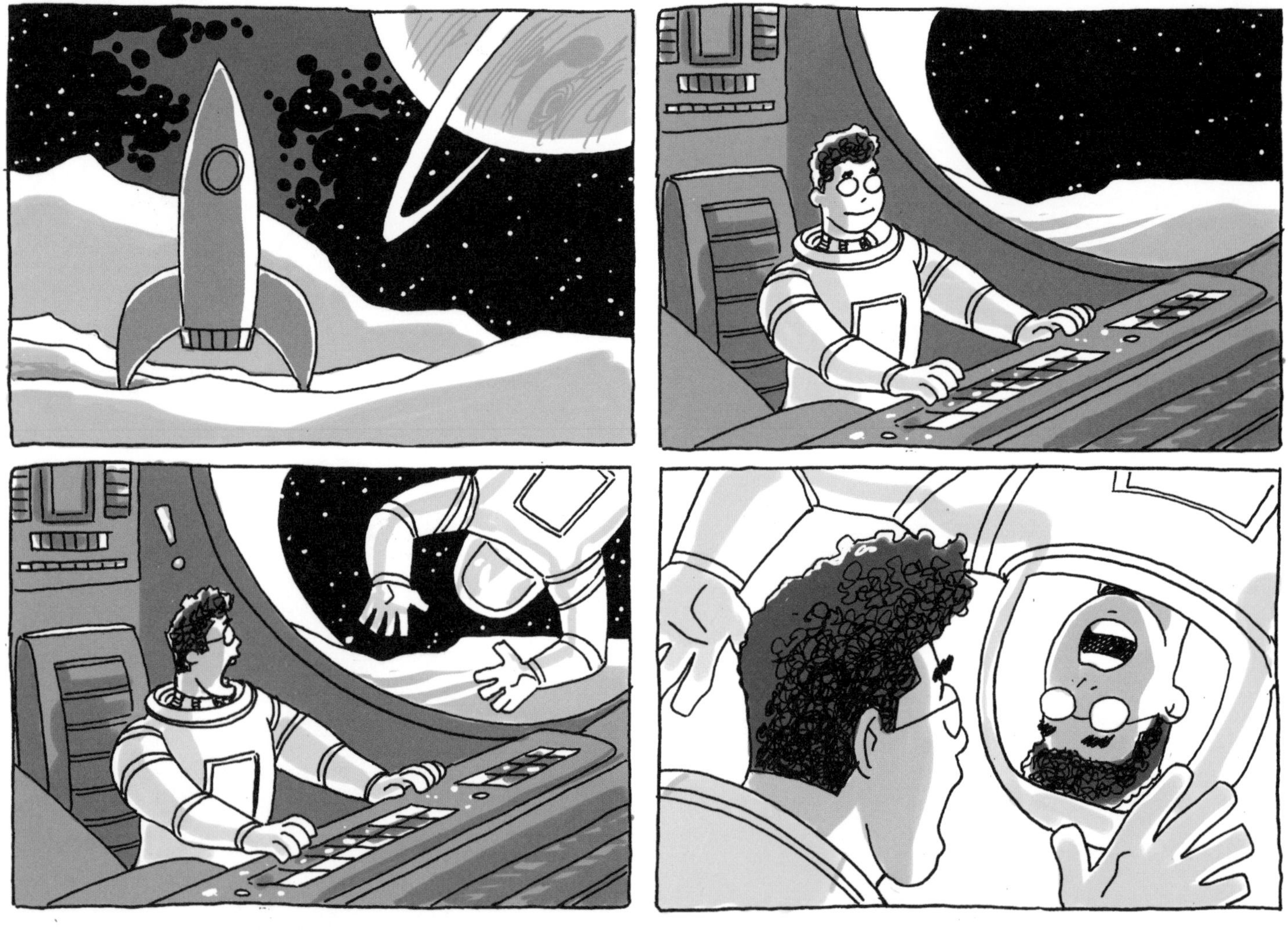

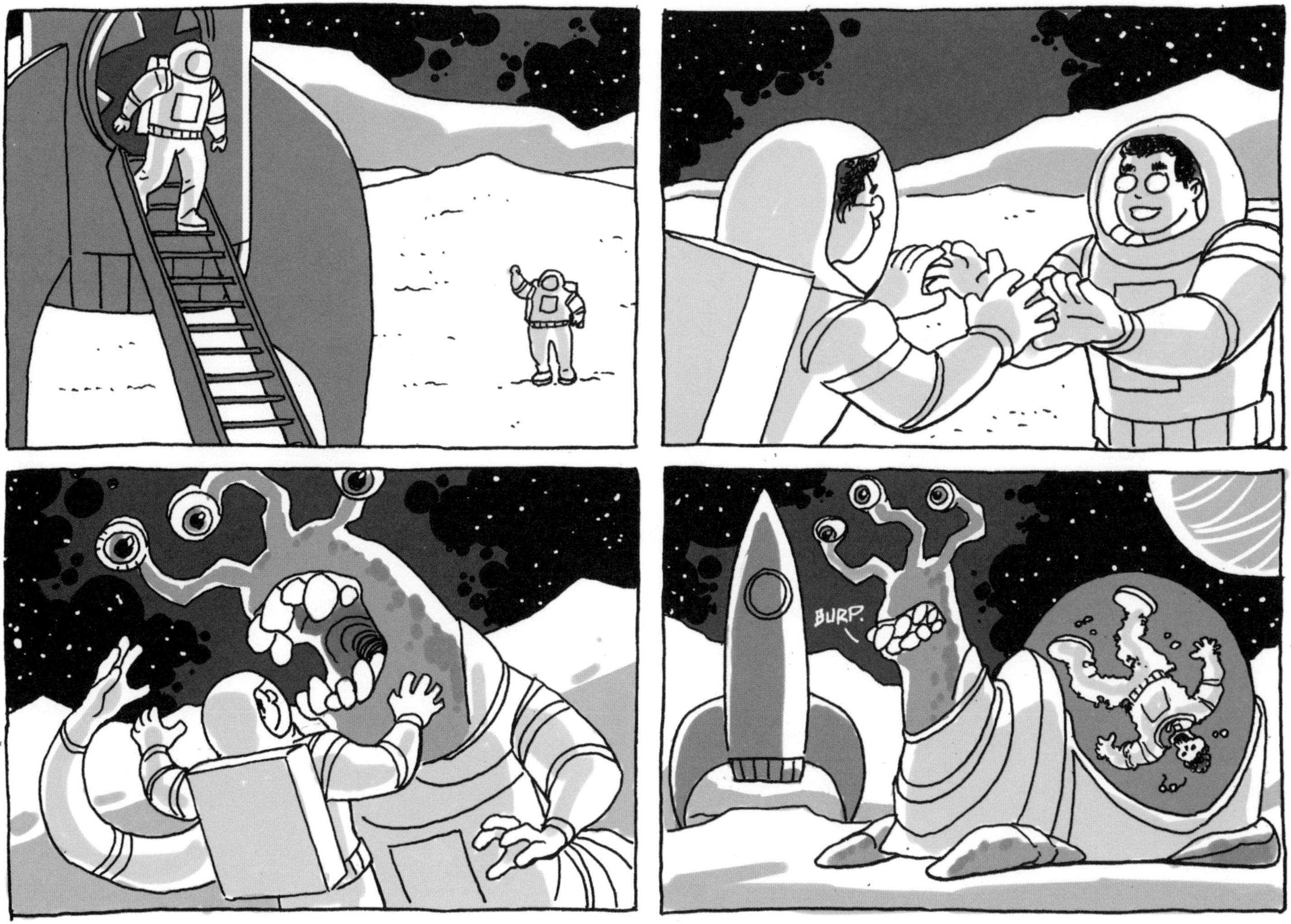
BURP.

THE PERILS OF LITERATURE

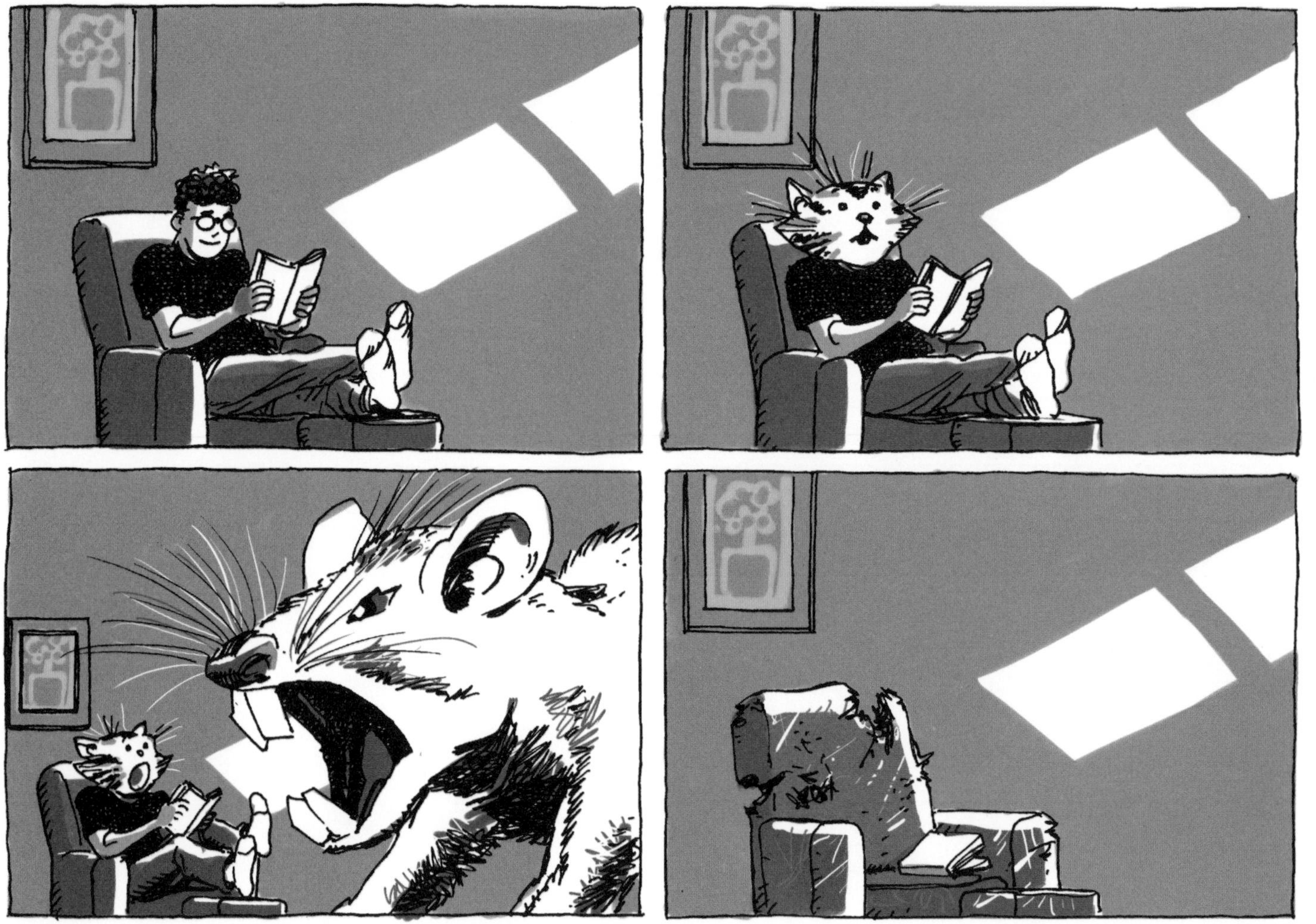

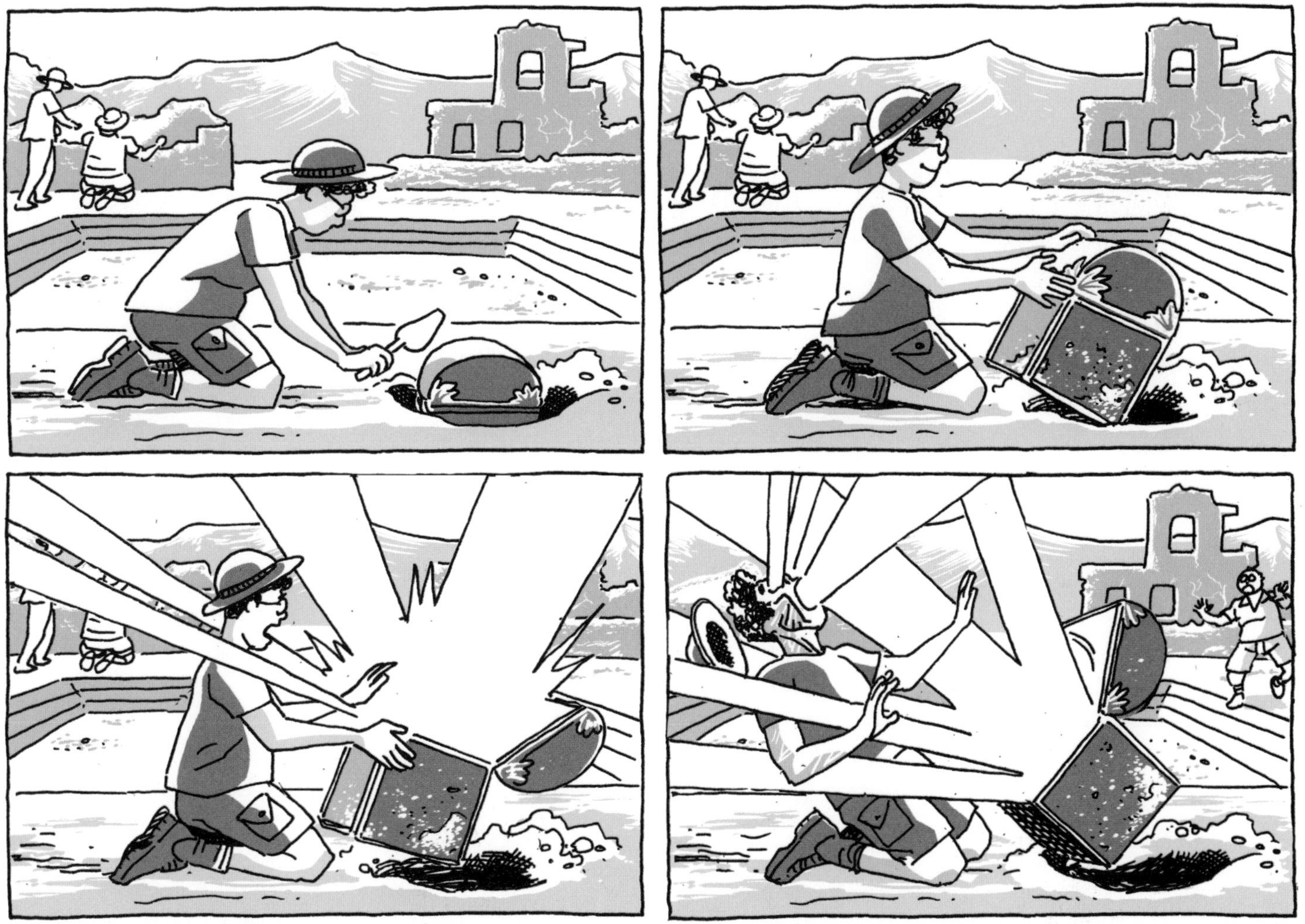

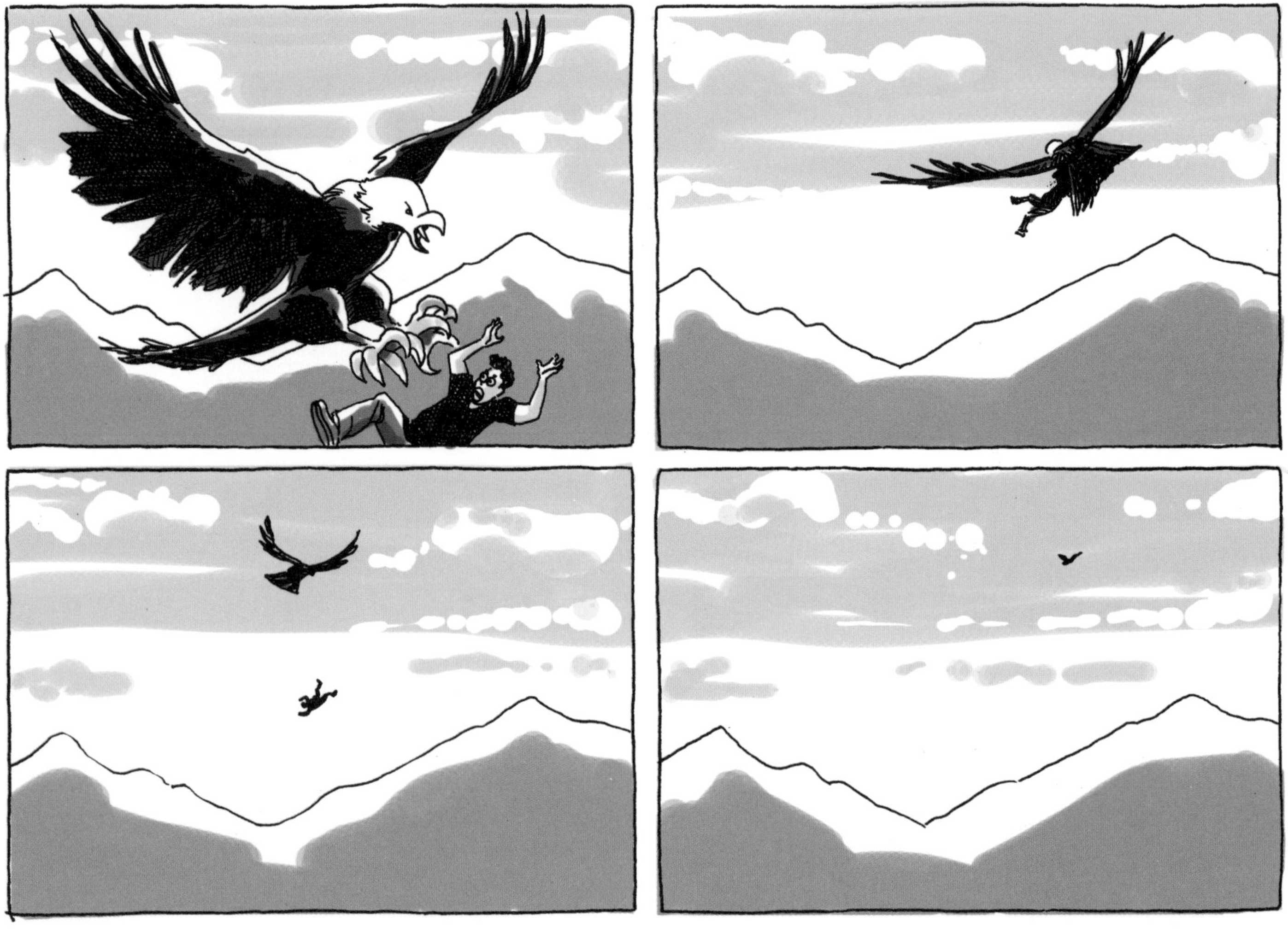

B FLAT

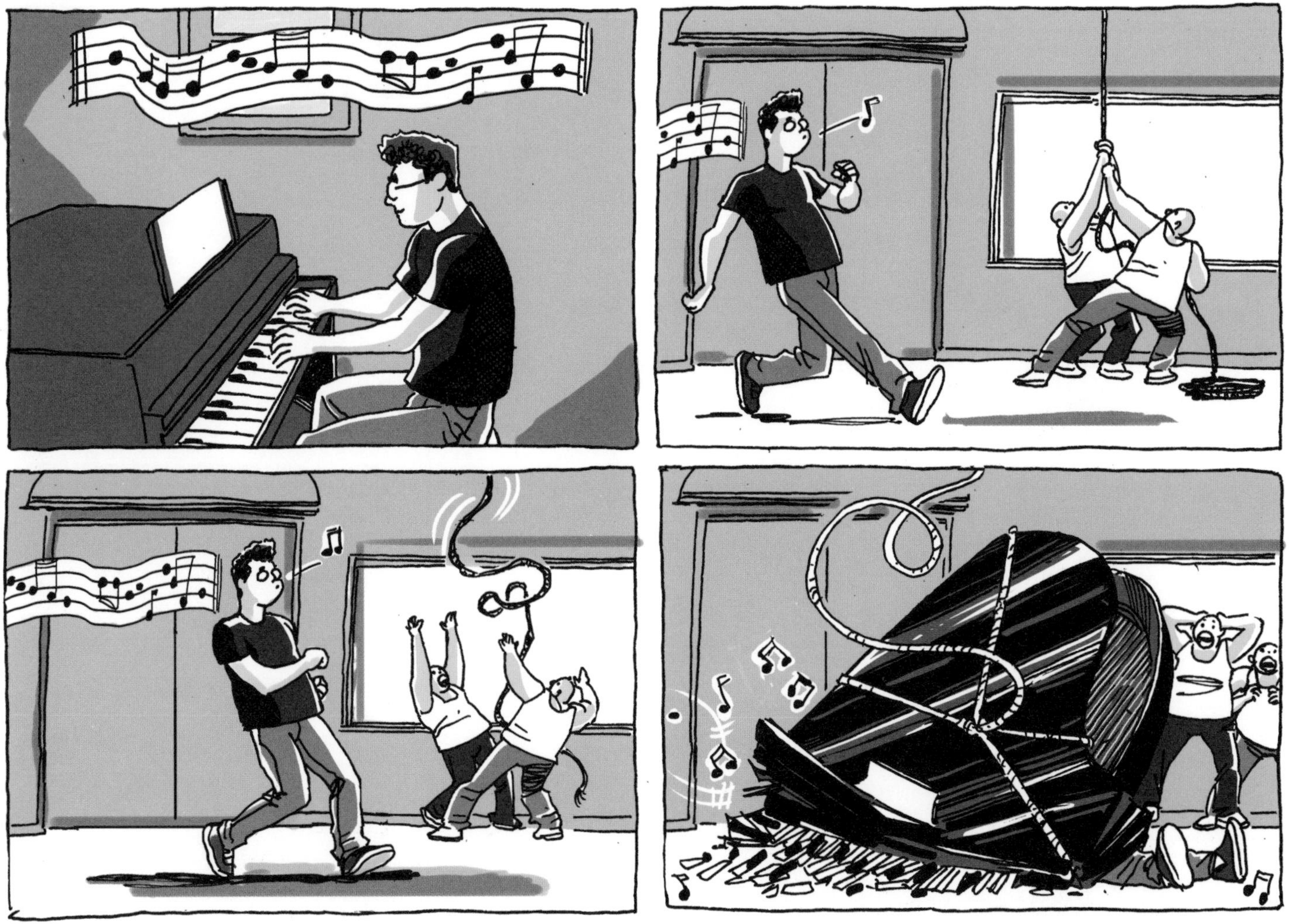

ALMOST THER_

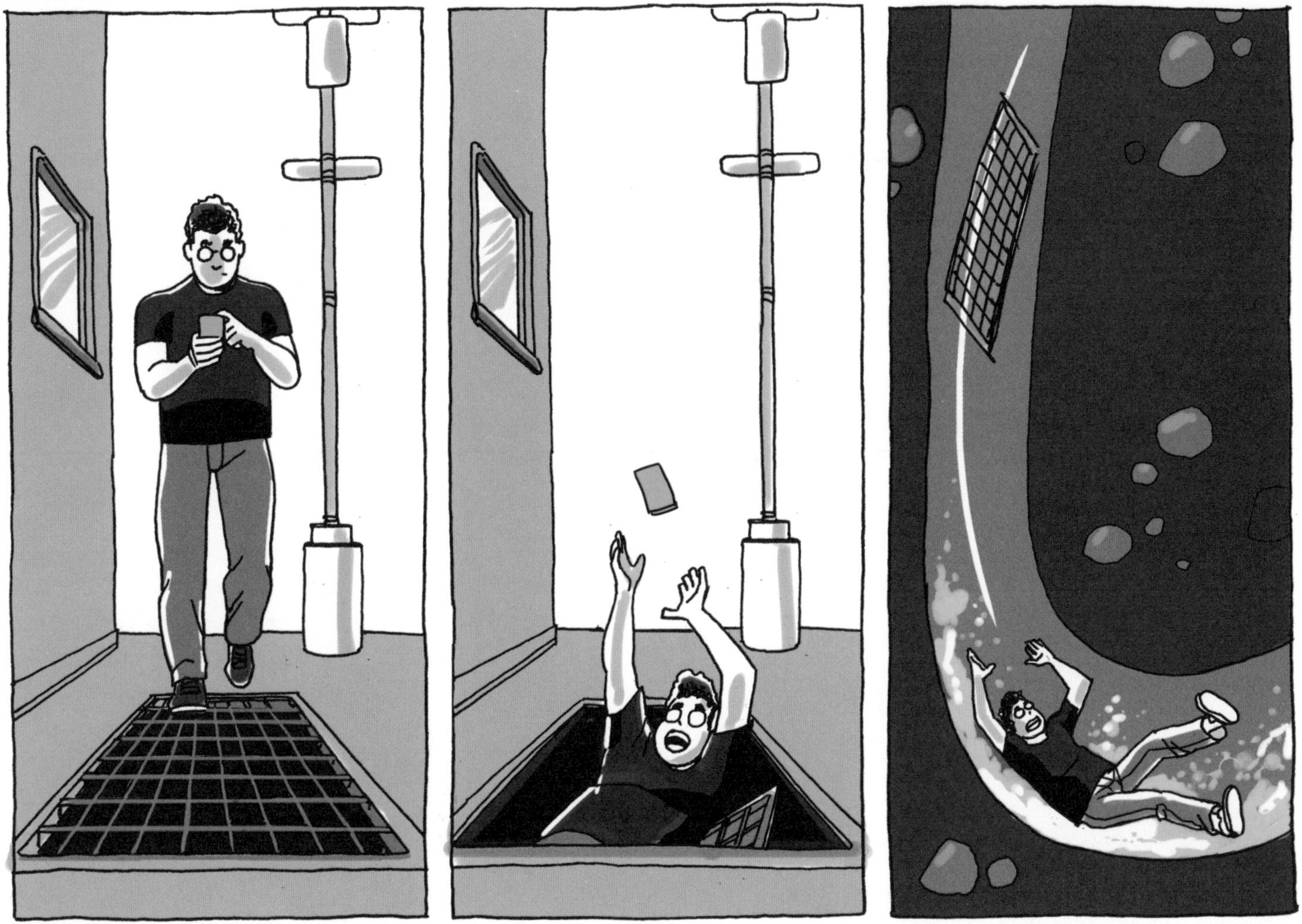

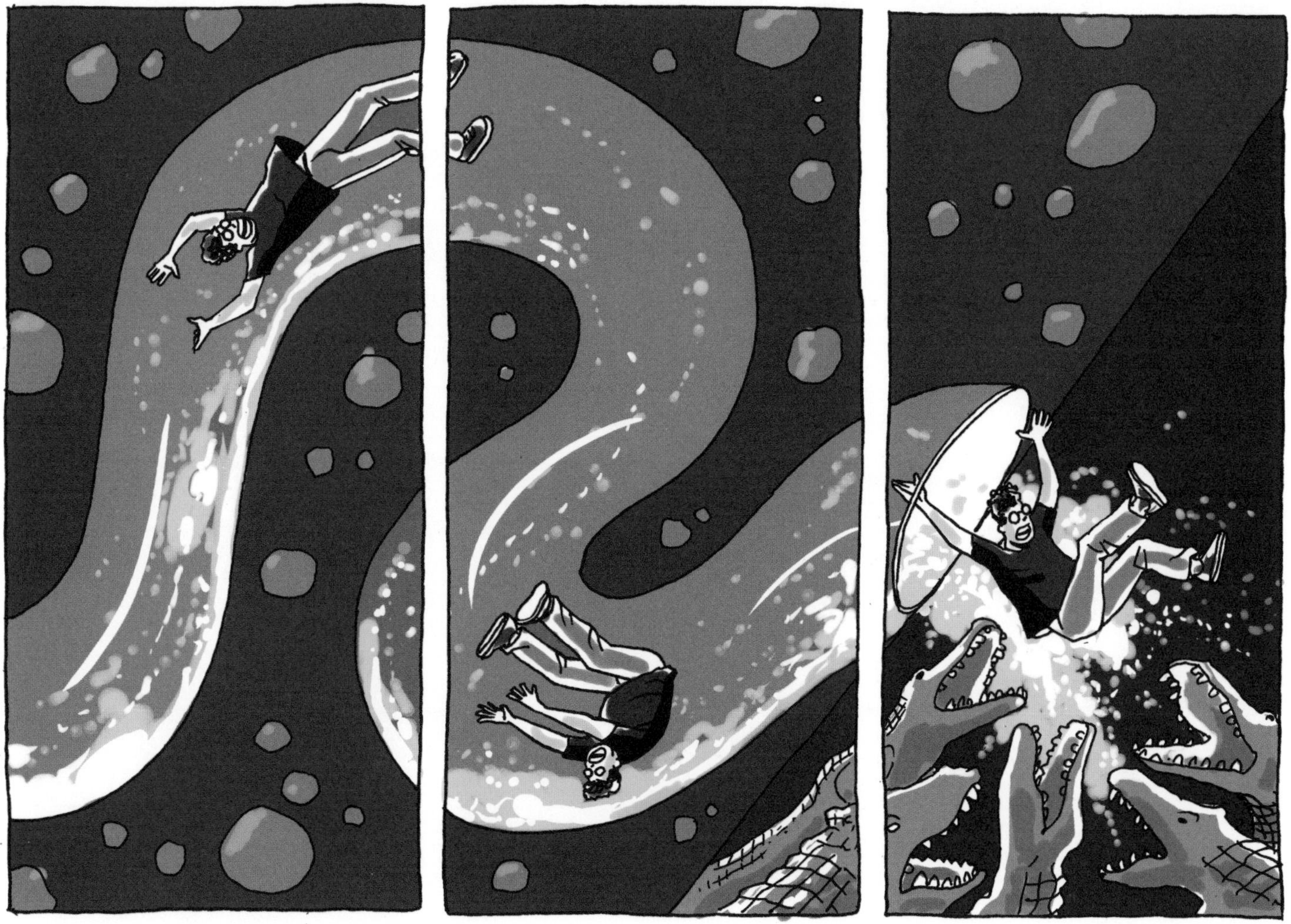

MEET THE ARTIST

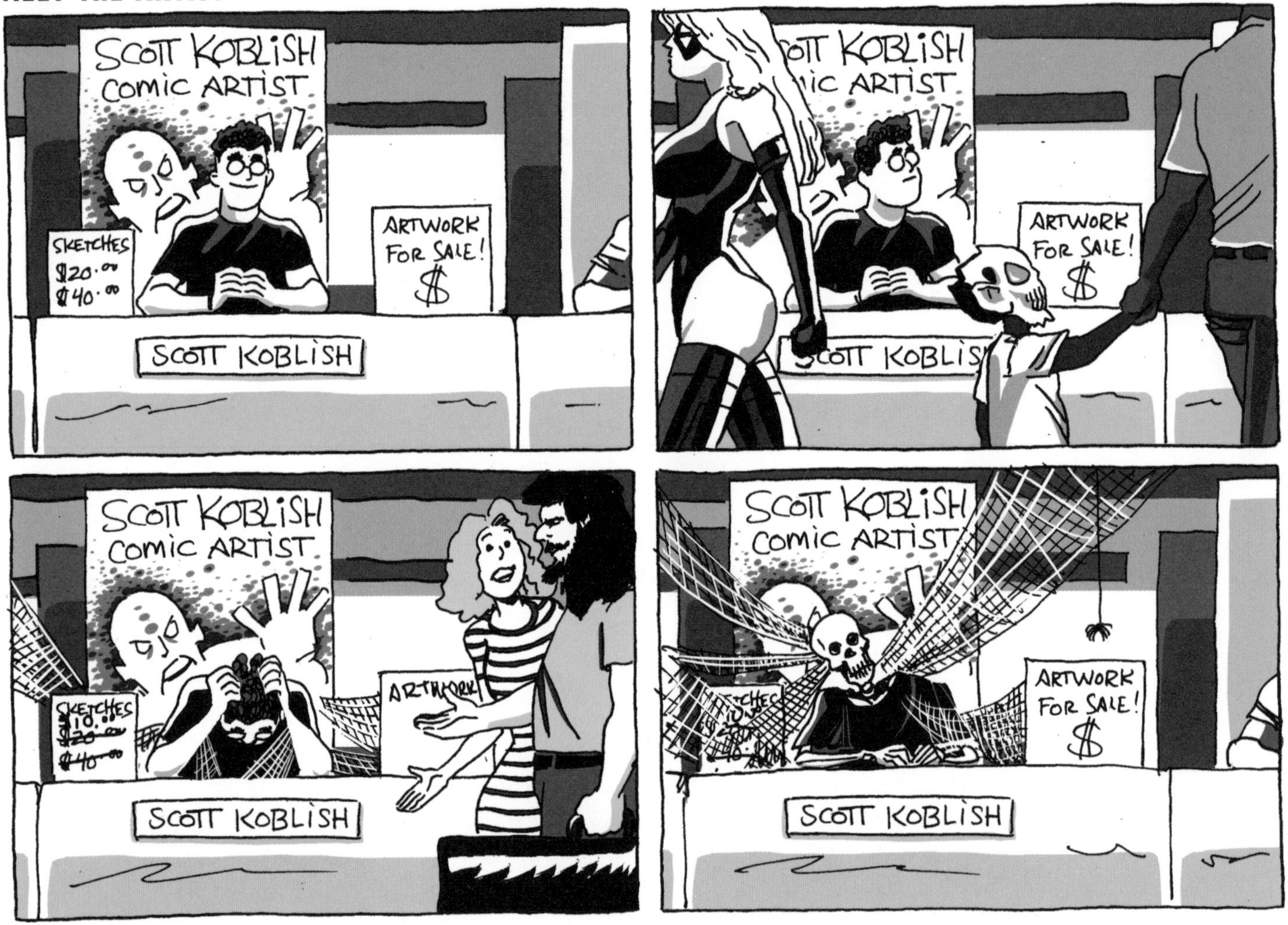

SCOTT KOBLISH
COMIC ARTIST
SKETCHES
$20.00
$40.00
ARTWORK
FOR SALE!
$
SCOTT KOBLISH
ARTWORK
FOR SALE!
$
SCOTT KOBLISH
COMIC ARTIST
SKETCHES
$10.00
$20.00
$40.00
ARTWORK
SCOTT KOBLISH
SCOTT KOBLISH
COMIC ARTIST
ARTWORK
FOR SALE!
$
SCOTT KOBLISH

CHANGE COMES FROM WITHIN

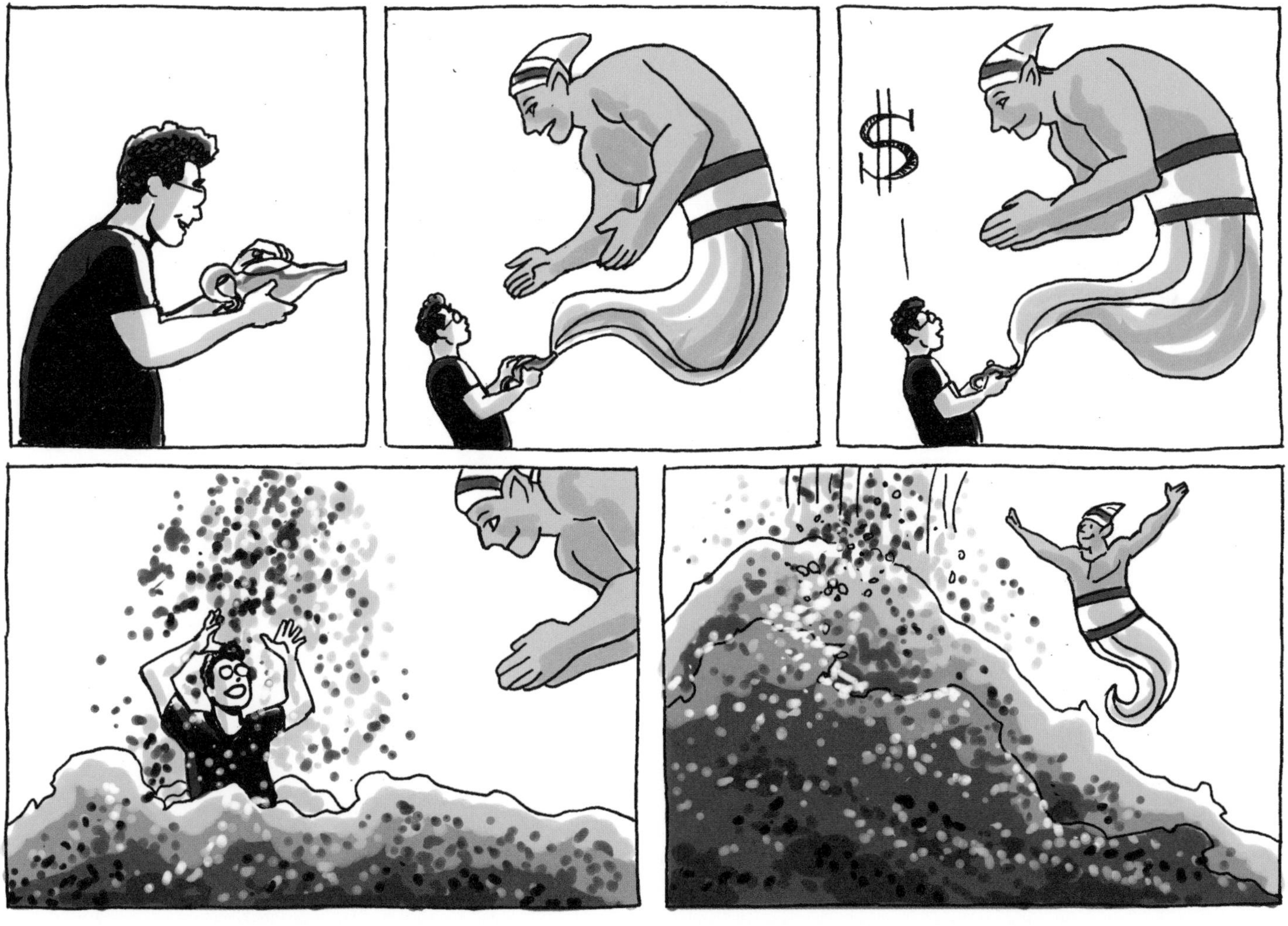
$

FEEDING THE PIGEONS

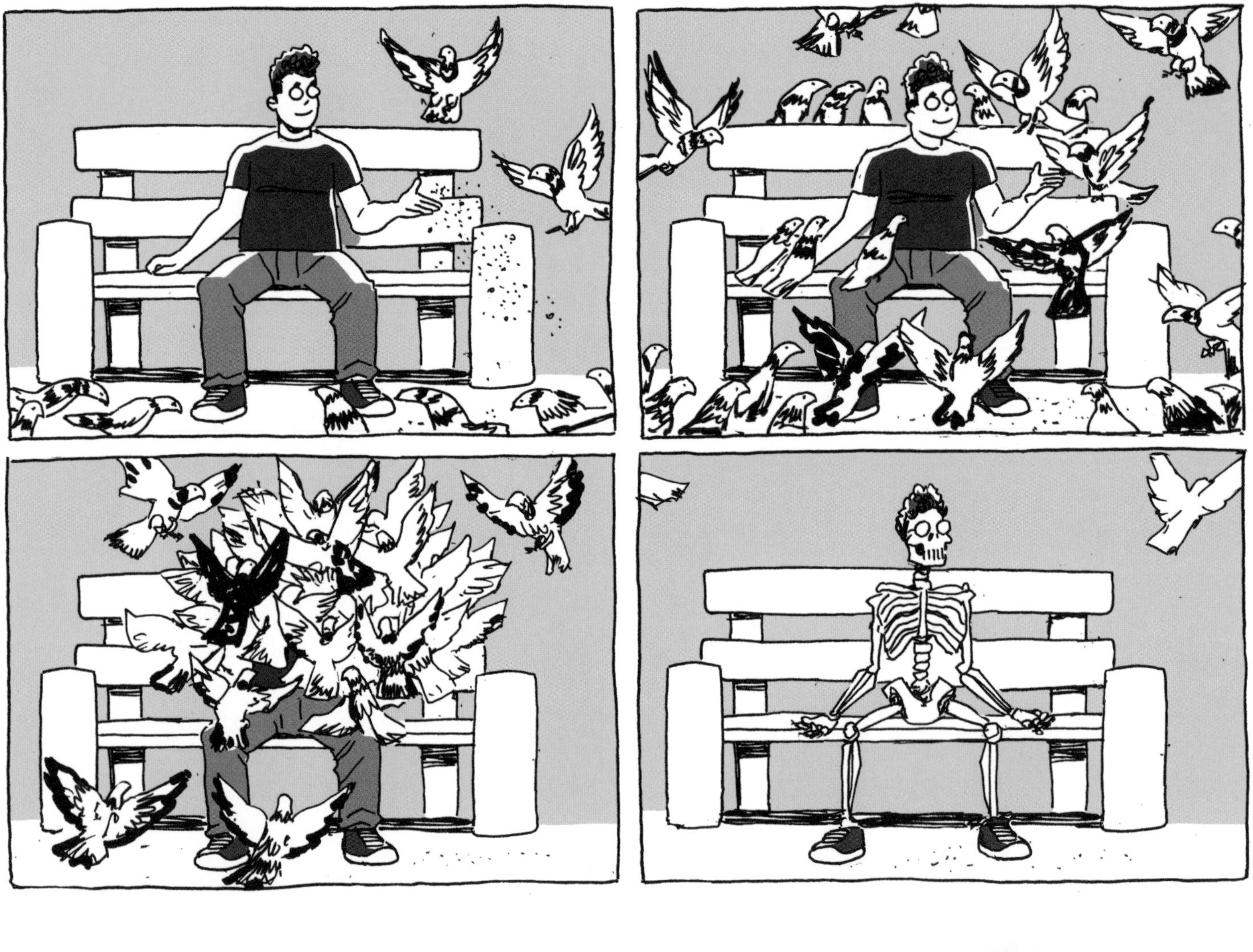

OOGA BOOGA

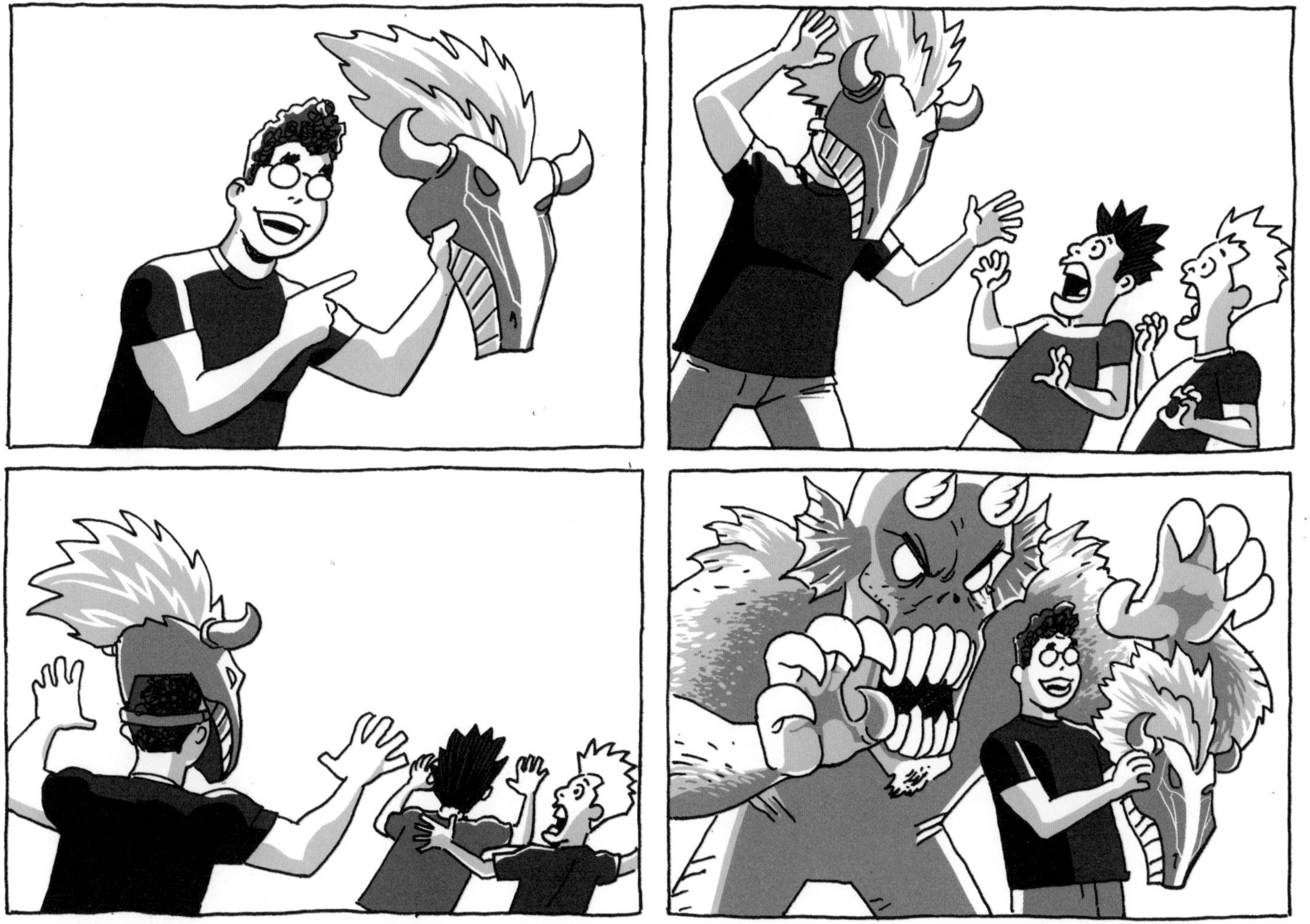

THE CHAMP

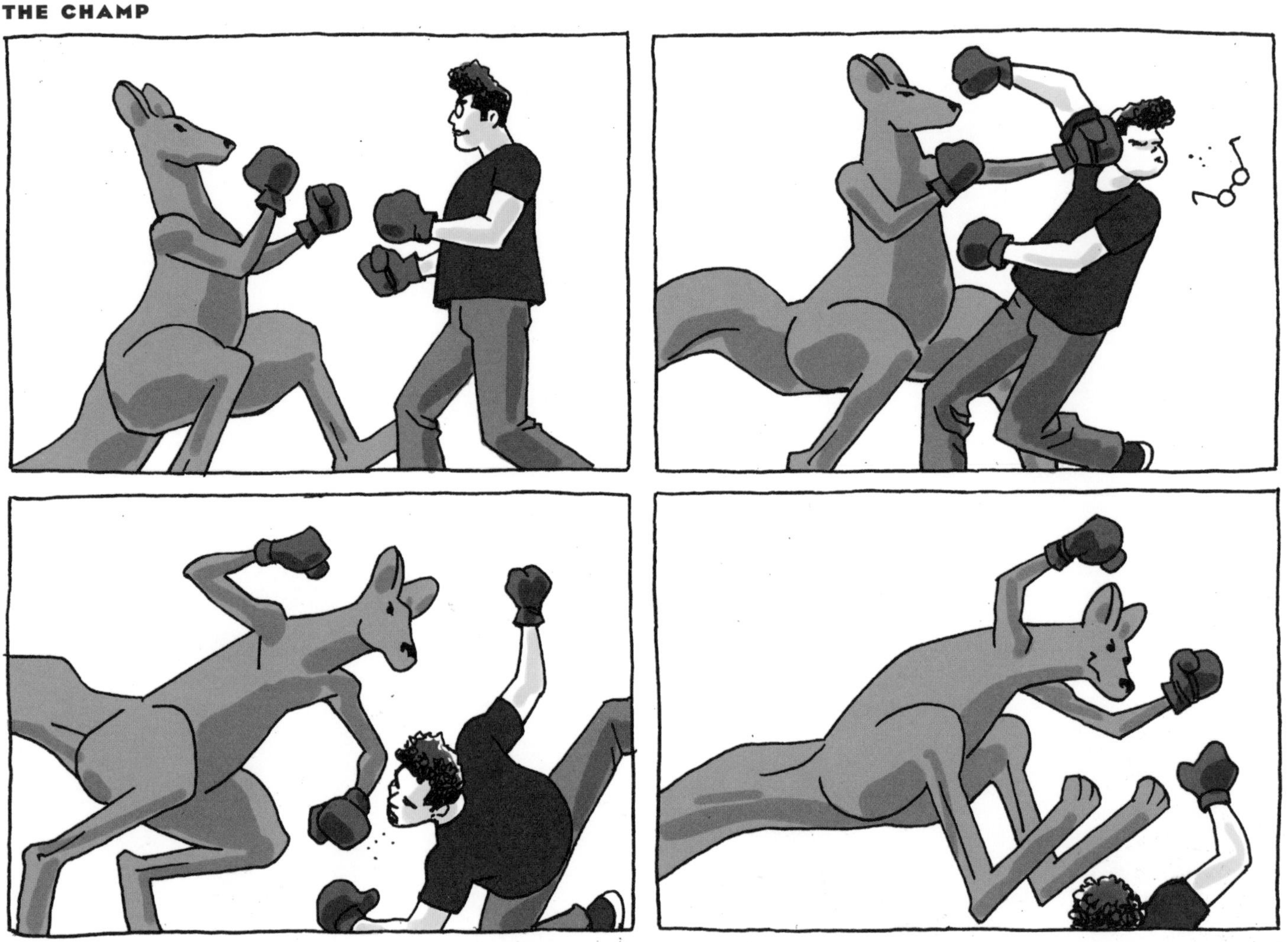

DORM DÉCOR

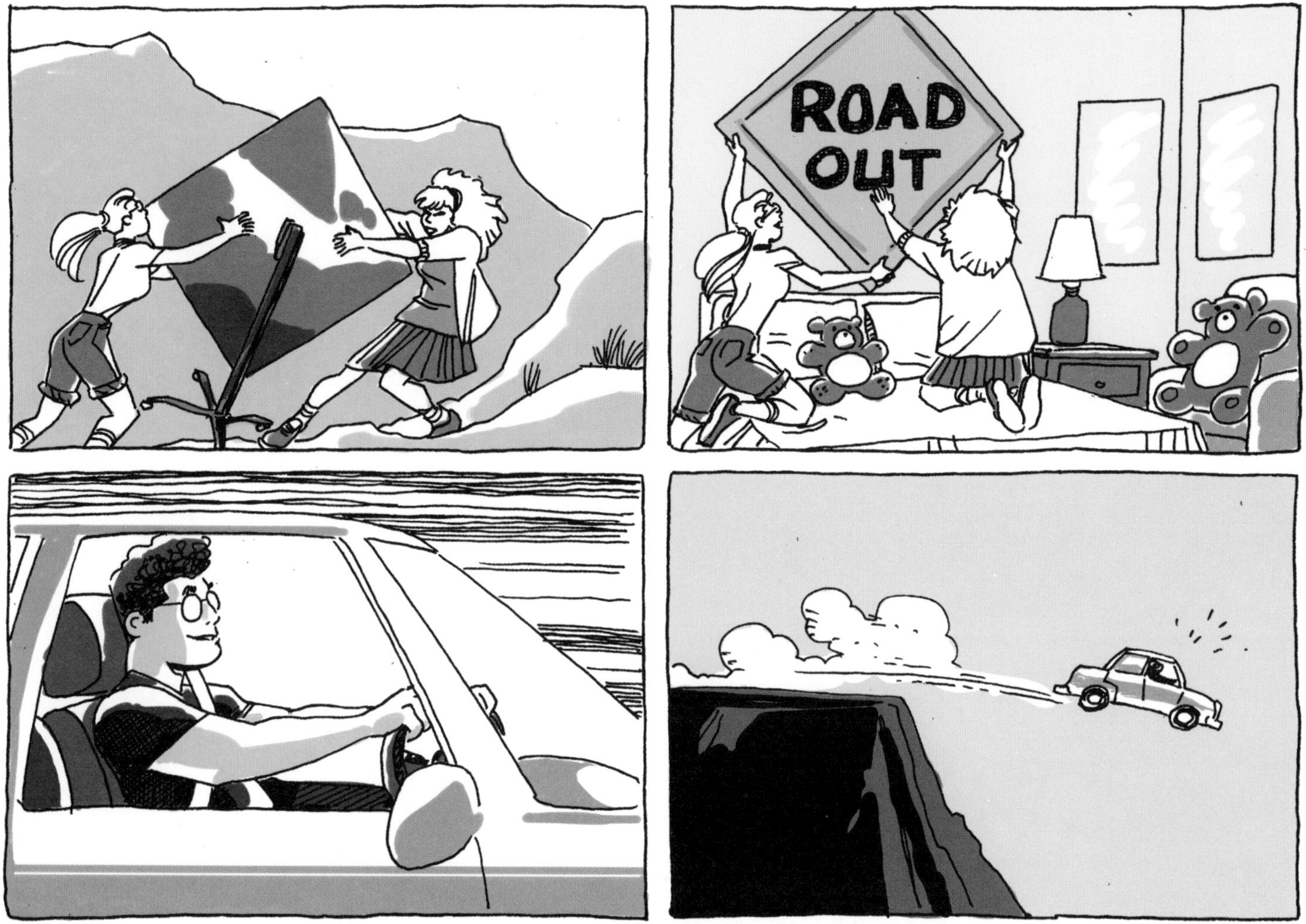
ROAD OUT

SPOILER ALERT

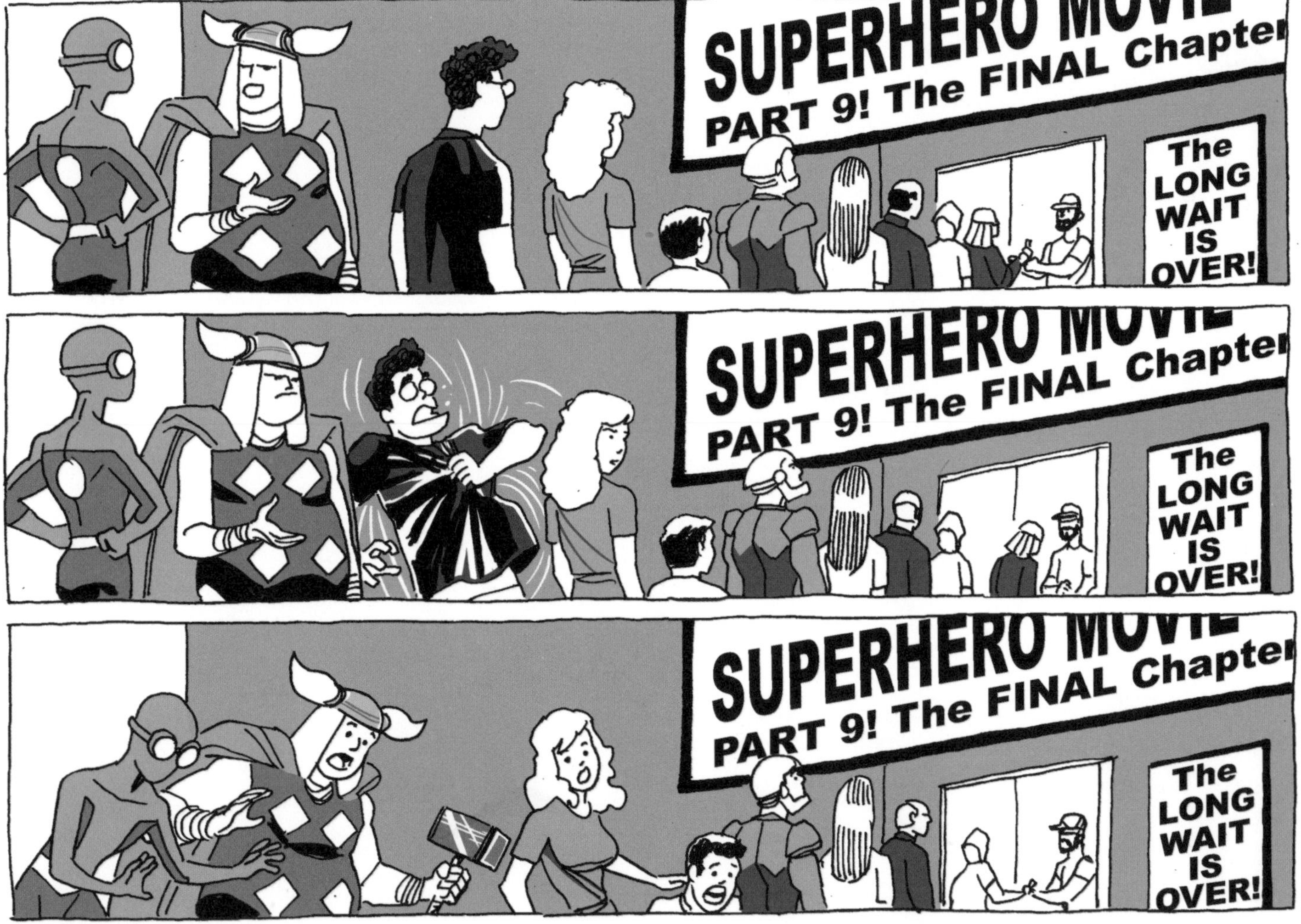

SUPERHERO
PART 9! The FINAL Chapte
The LONG WAIT IS OVER!
SUPERHERO
PART 9! The FINAL Chapte
The LONG WAIT IS OVER!
SUPERHERO
PART 9! The FINAL Chapte
The LONG WAIT IS OVER!

CRUISIN'

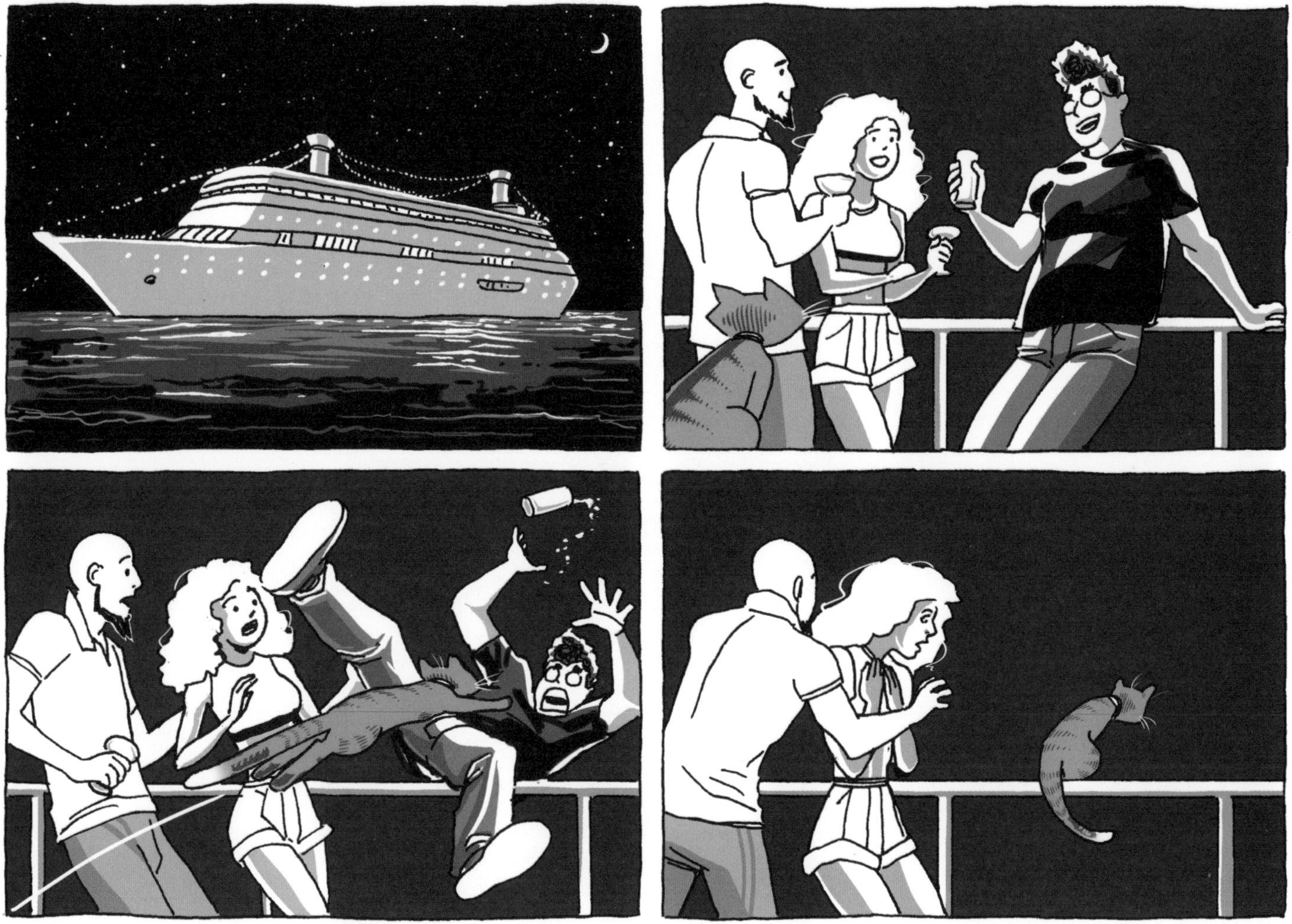

A REPRIEVE

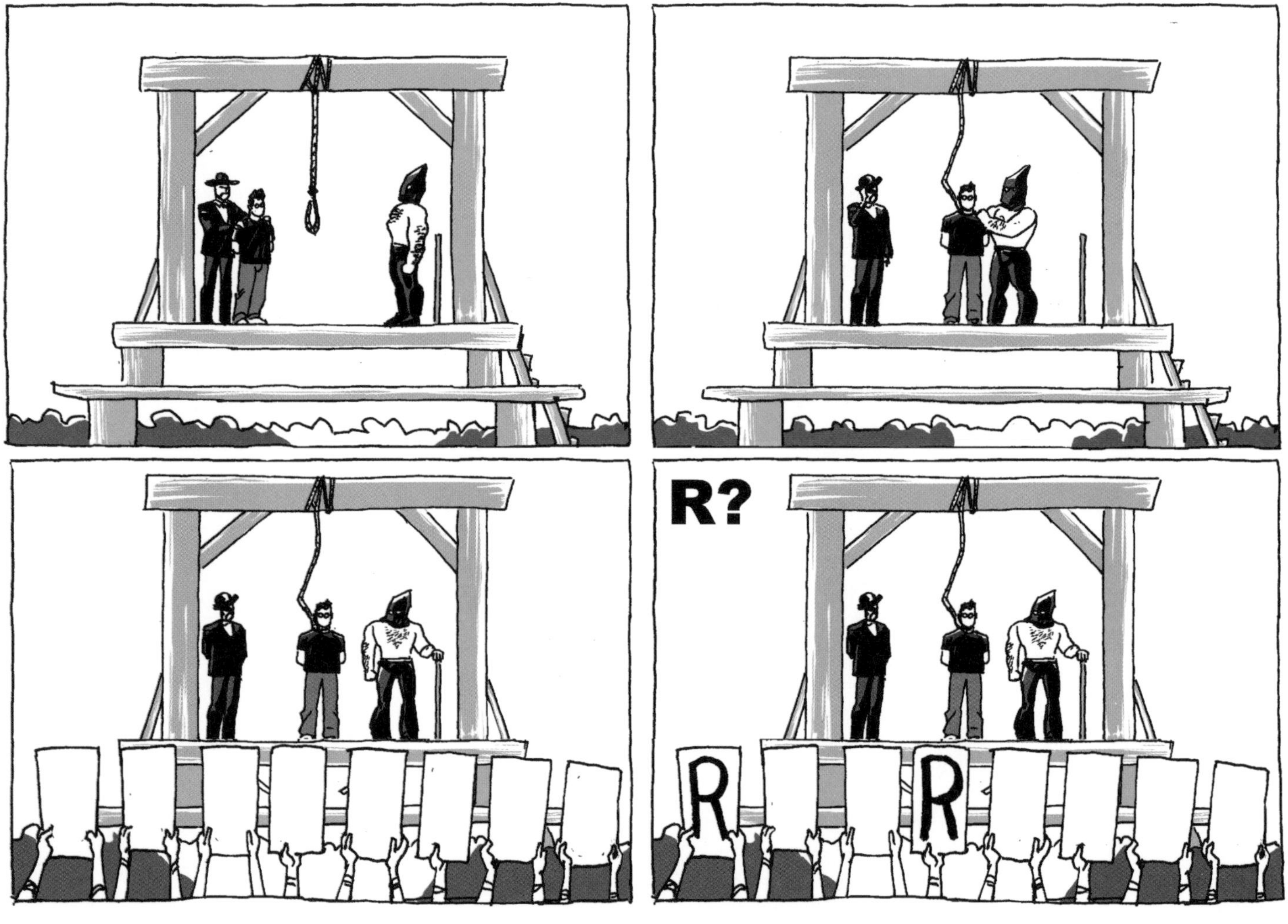
R?
R
R

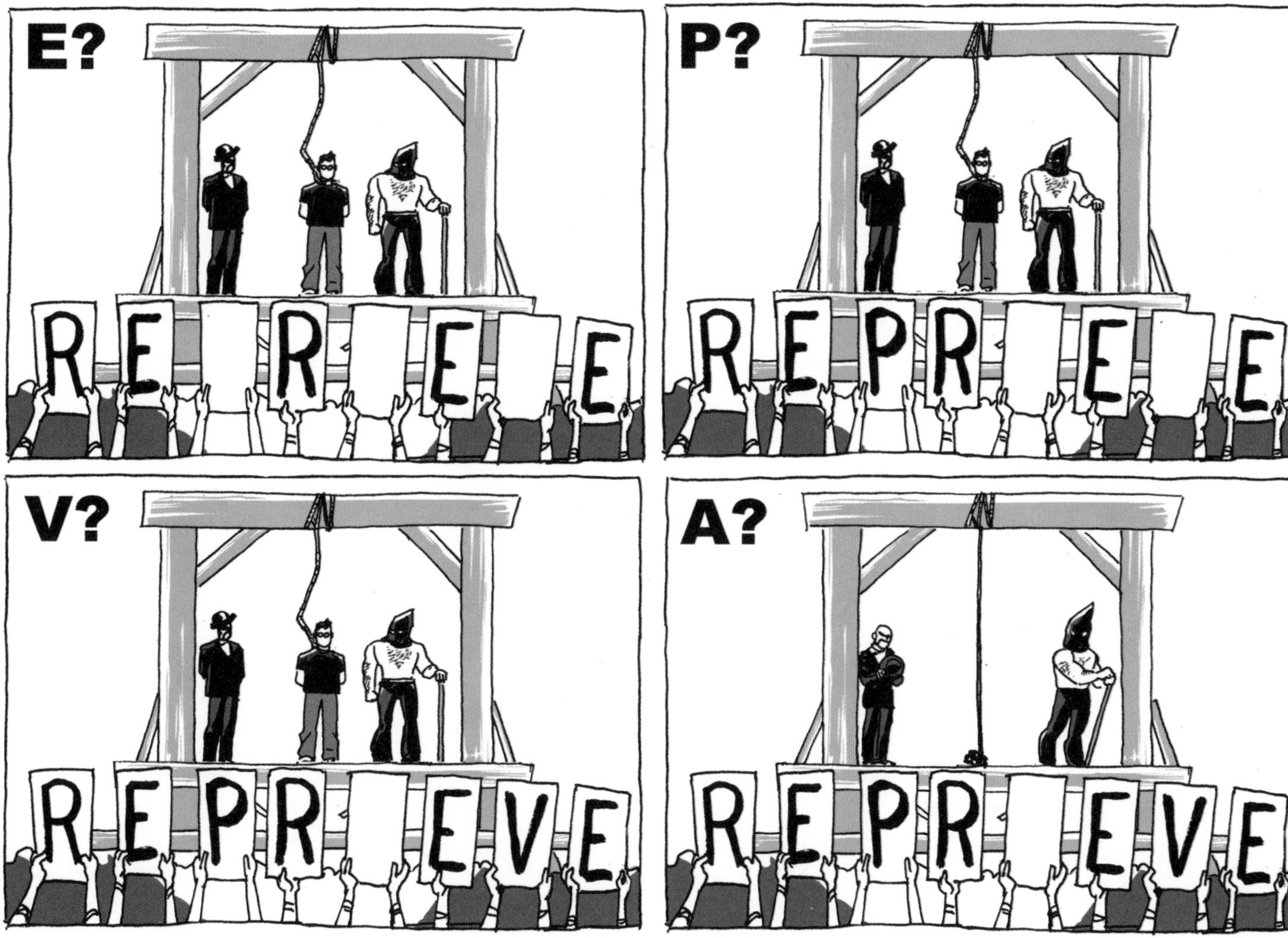
E?
RE R E E
P?
REPR E E
V?
REPR EVE
A?
REPR EVE

COOTIES

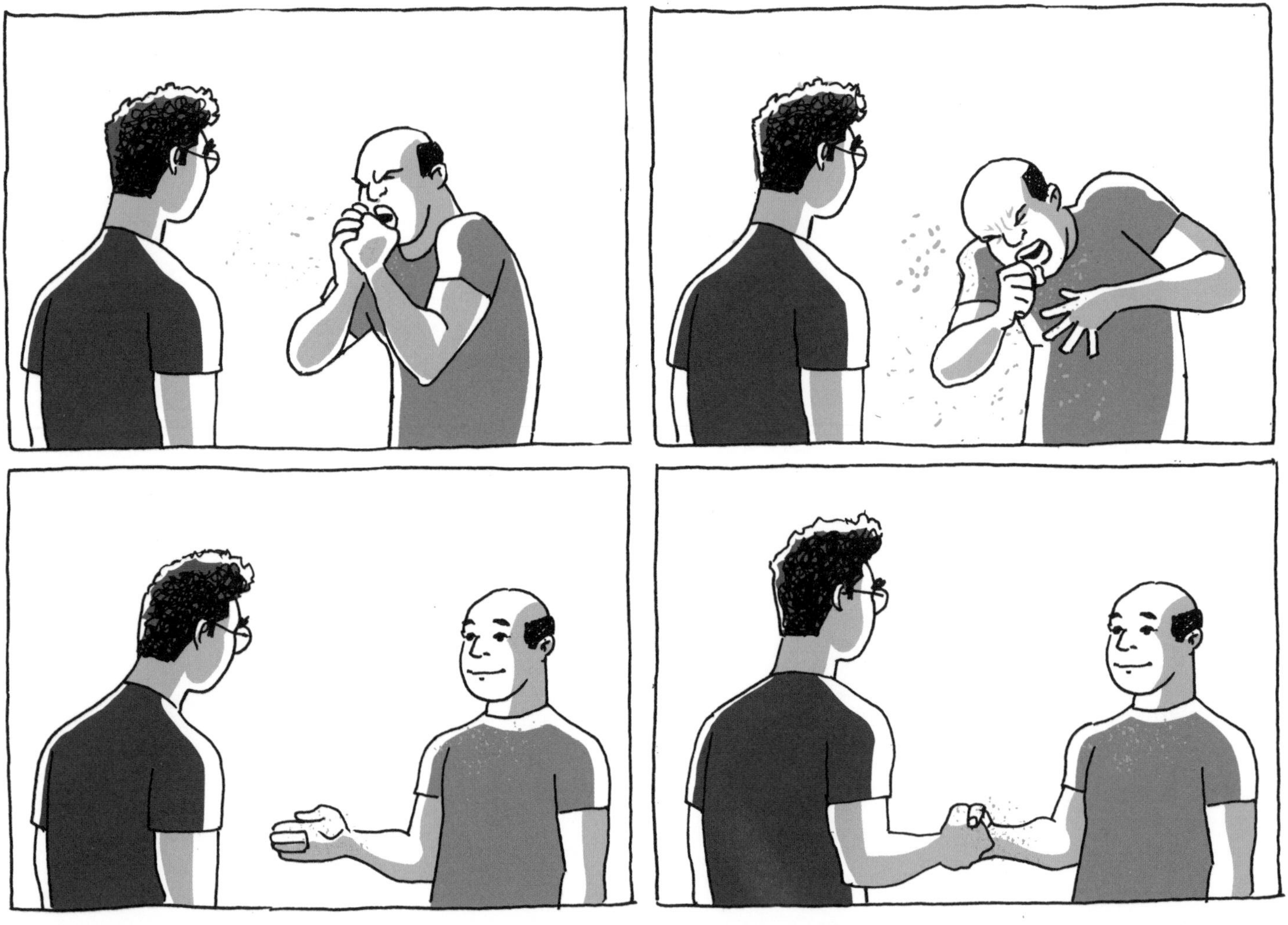

HAPPY BIRTHDAY

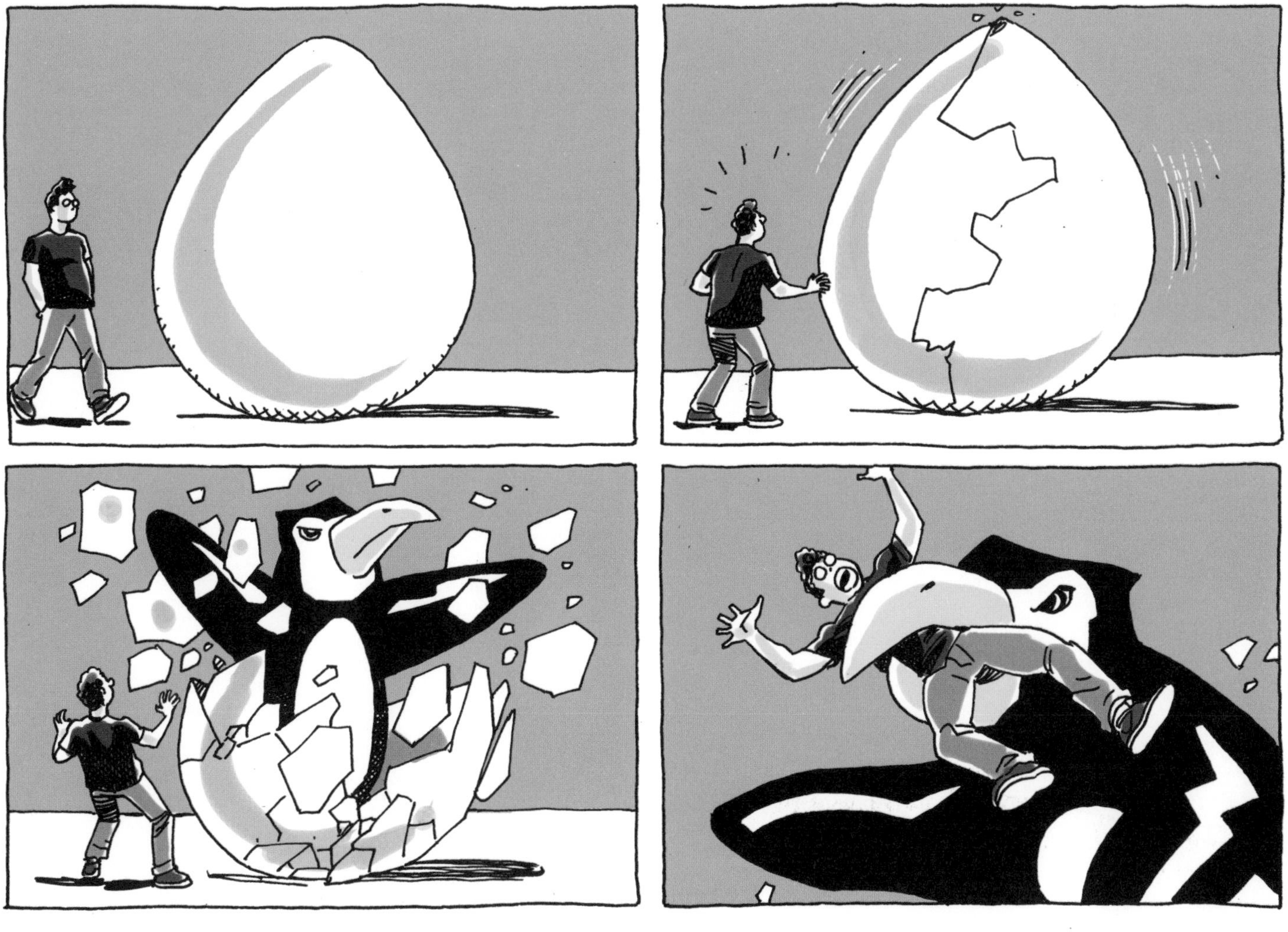

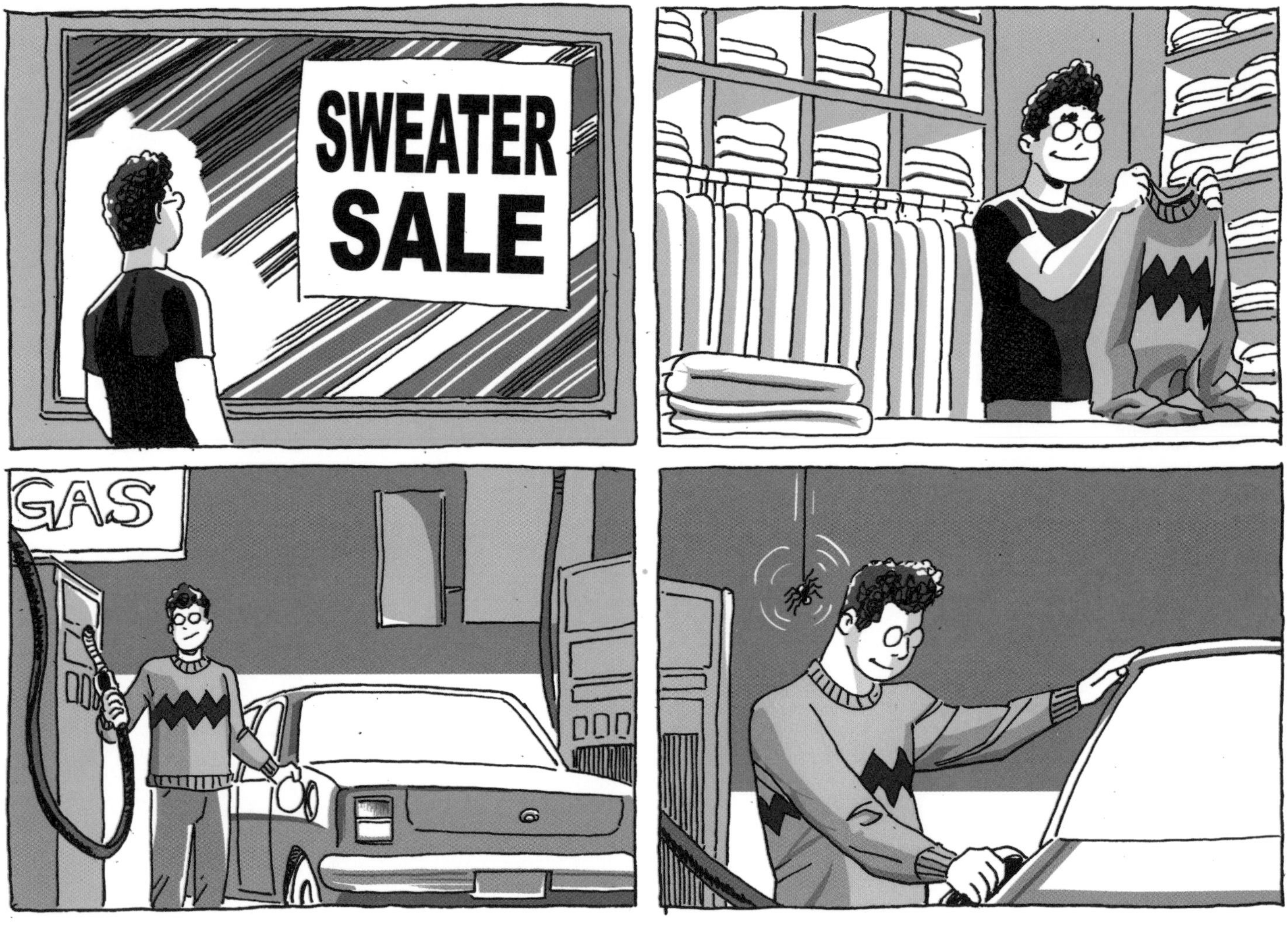
SWEATER
SALE
GAS

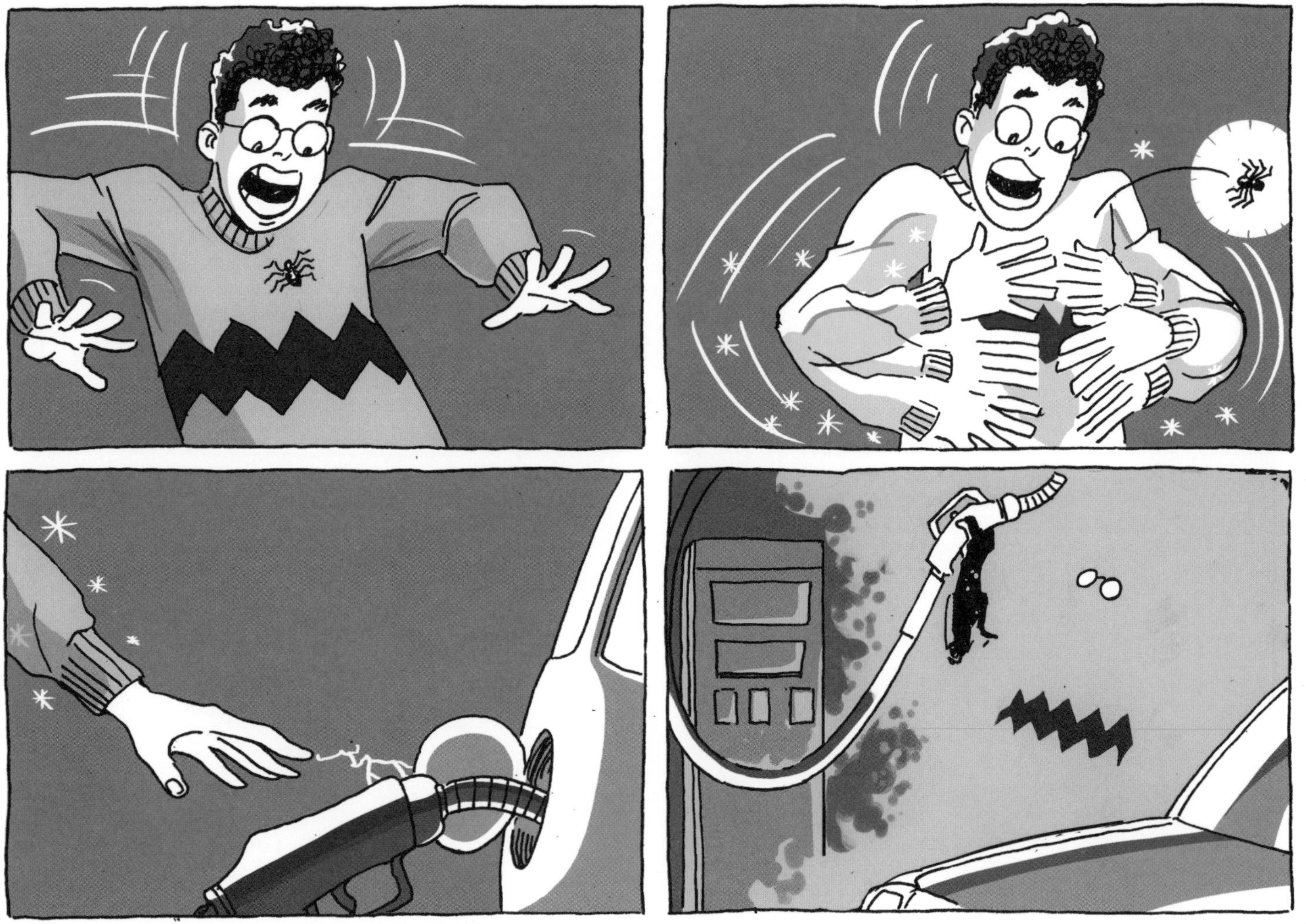

BRAIN FOOD

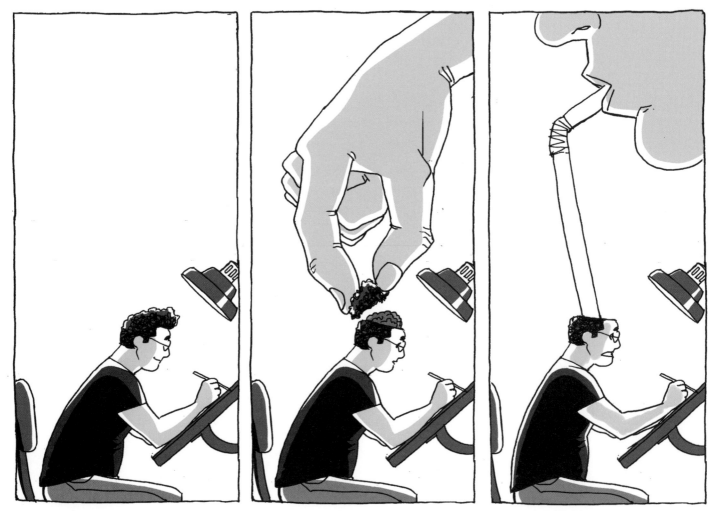

SCOTT BOT

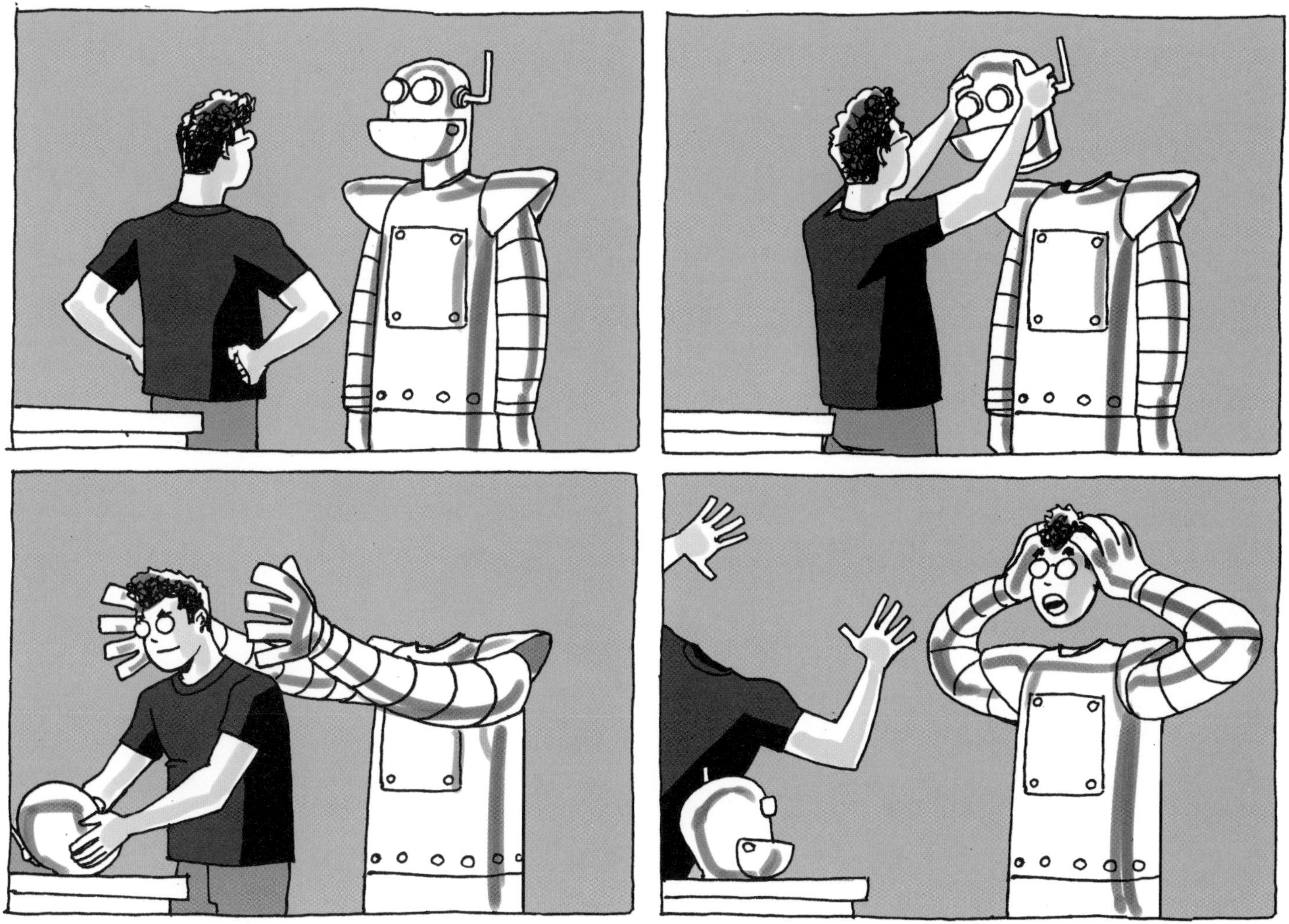

TWINKLE TWINKLE

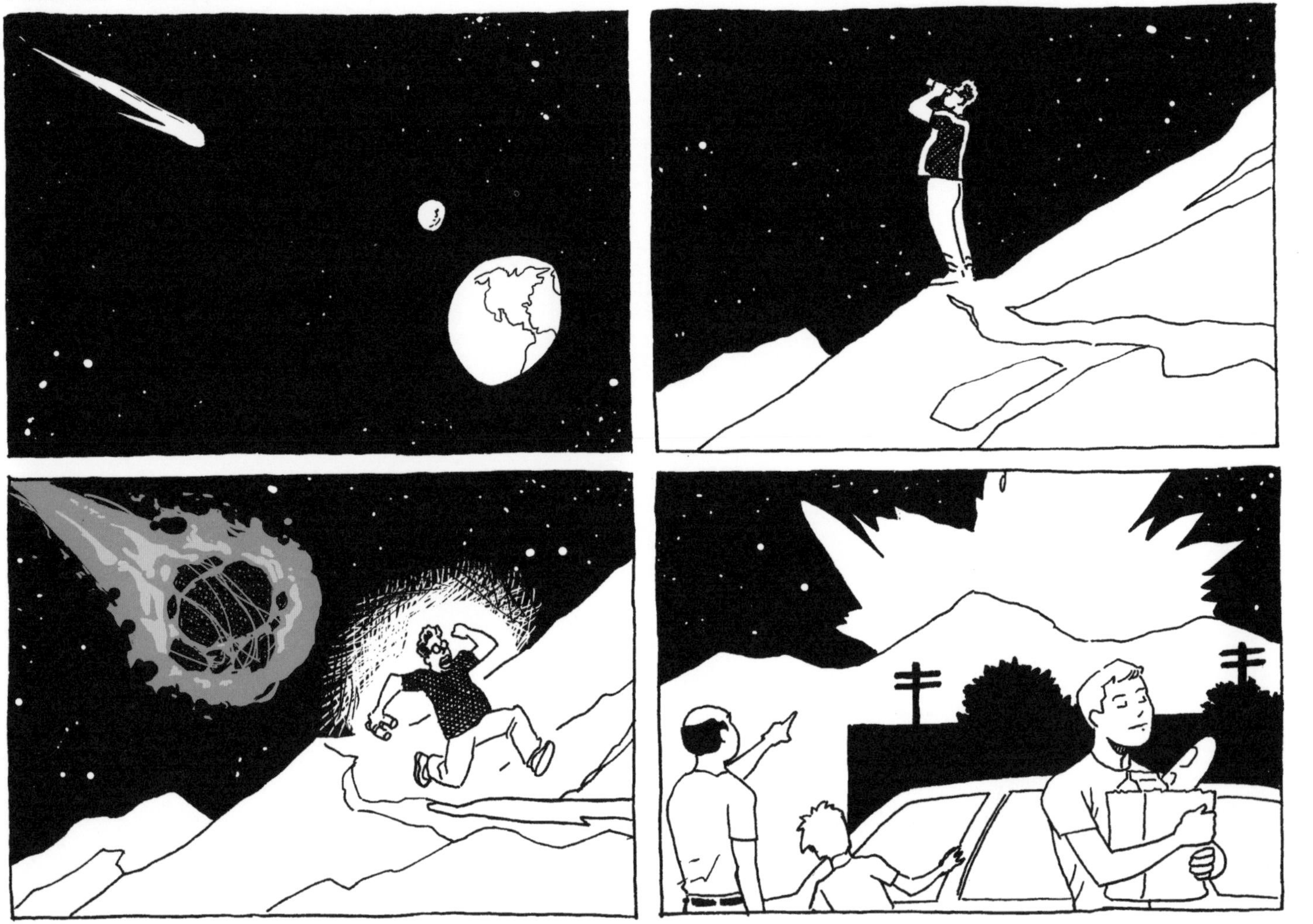

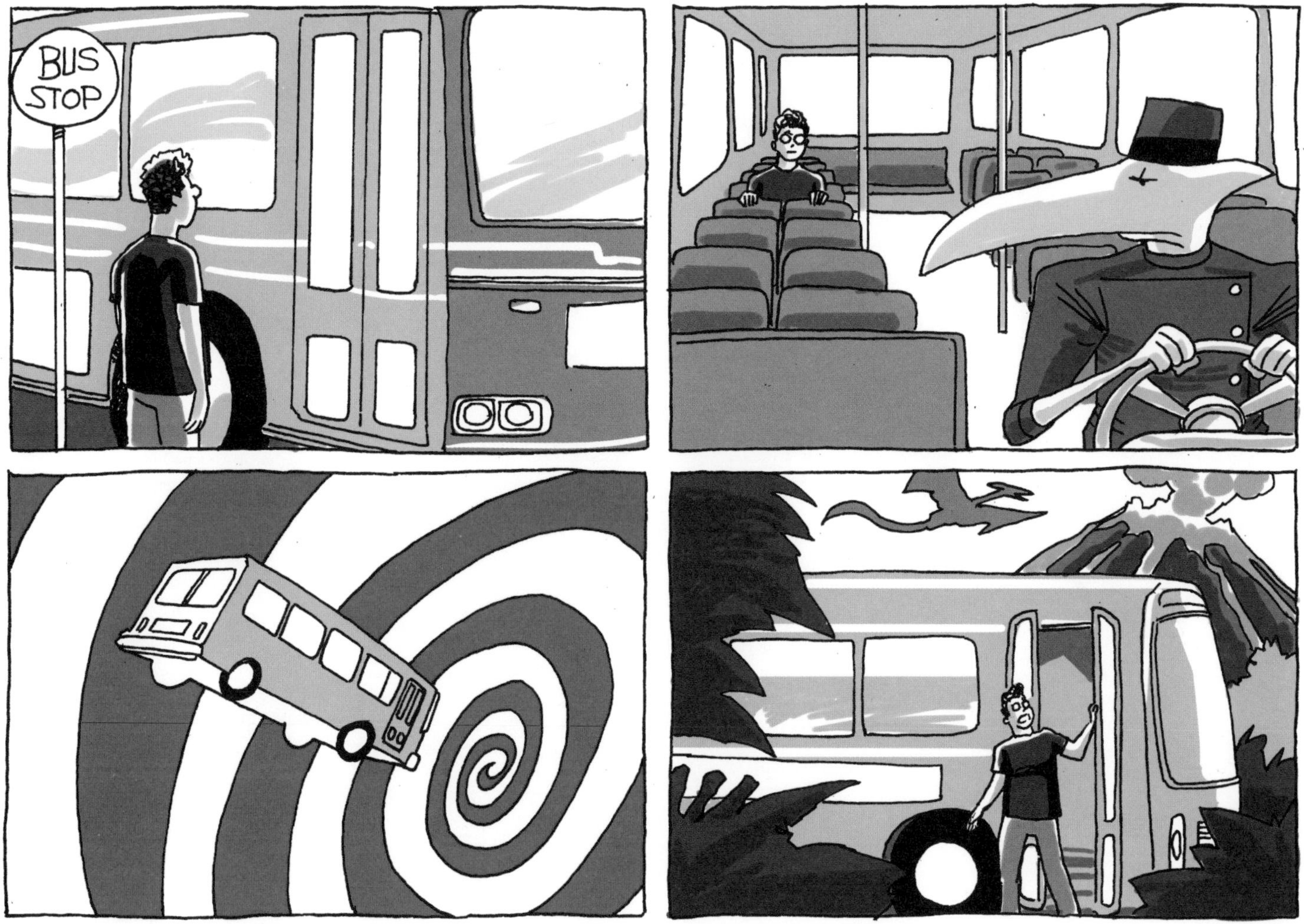
BUS
STOP

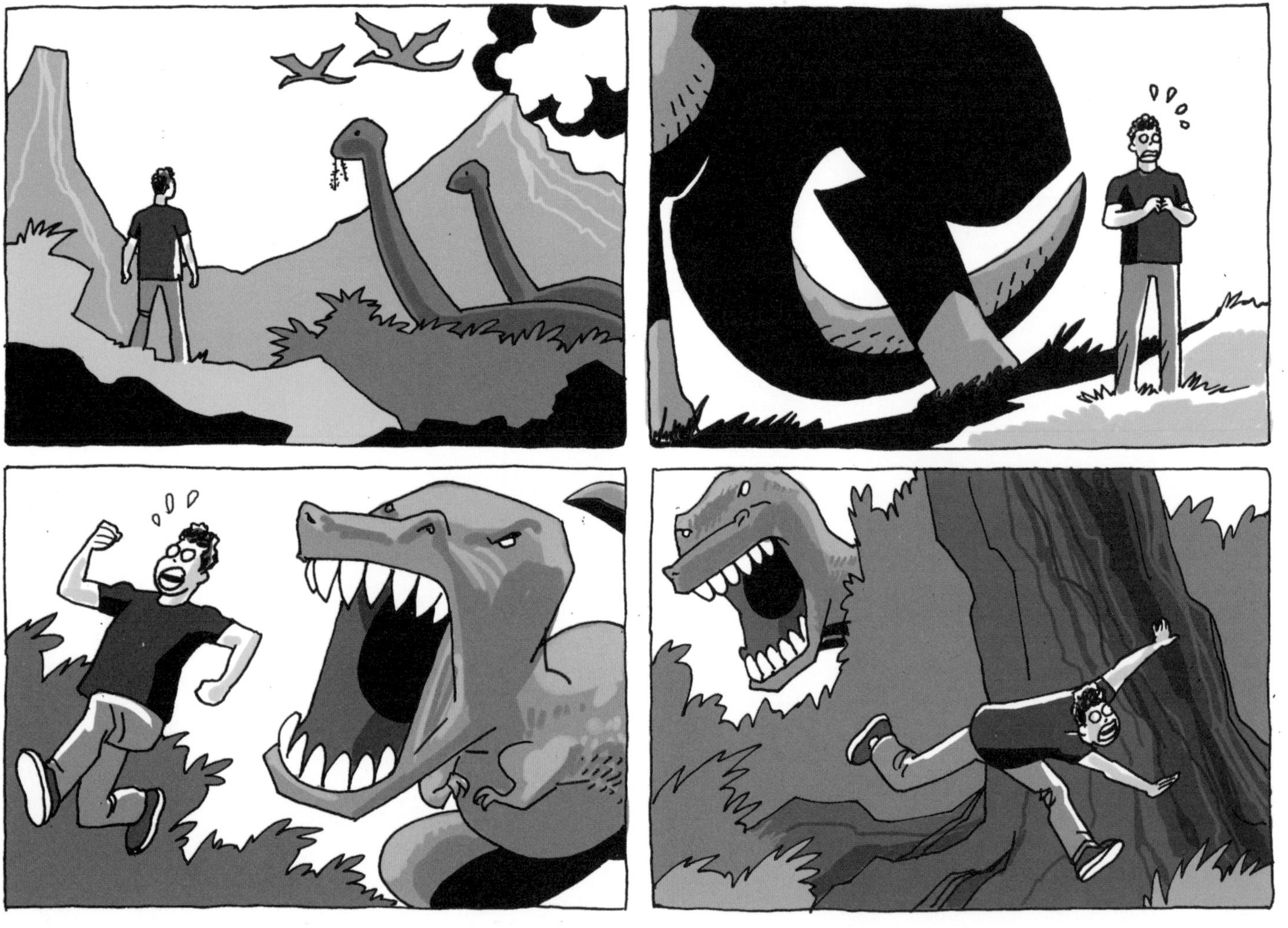

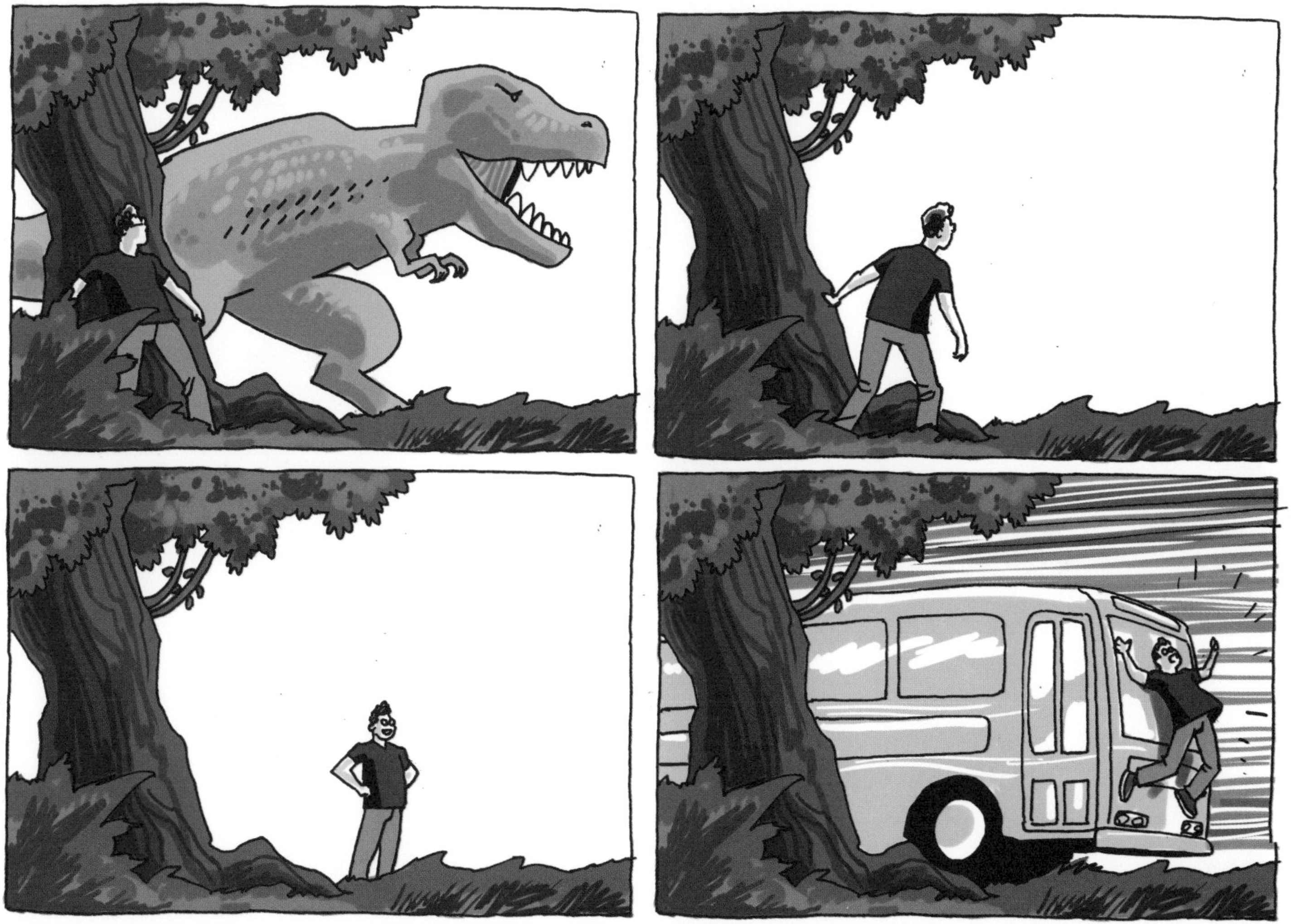

LAUNDRY DAY

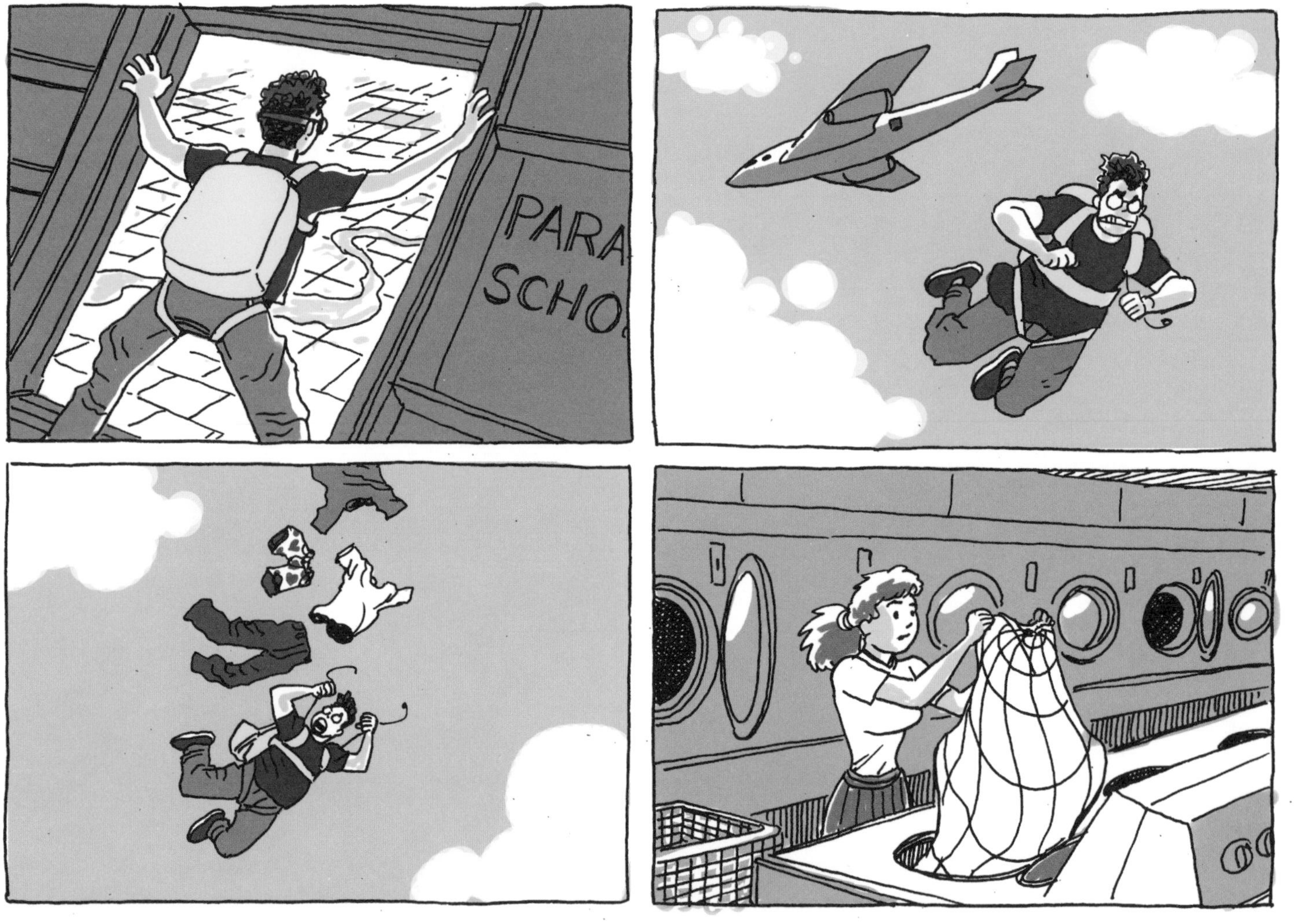

PARA
SCHO

FACTORY TOUR

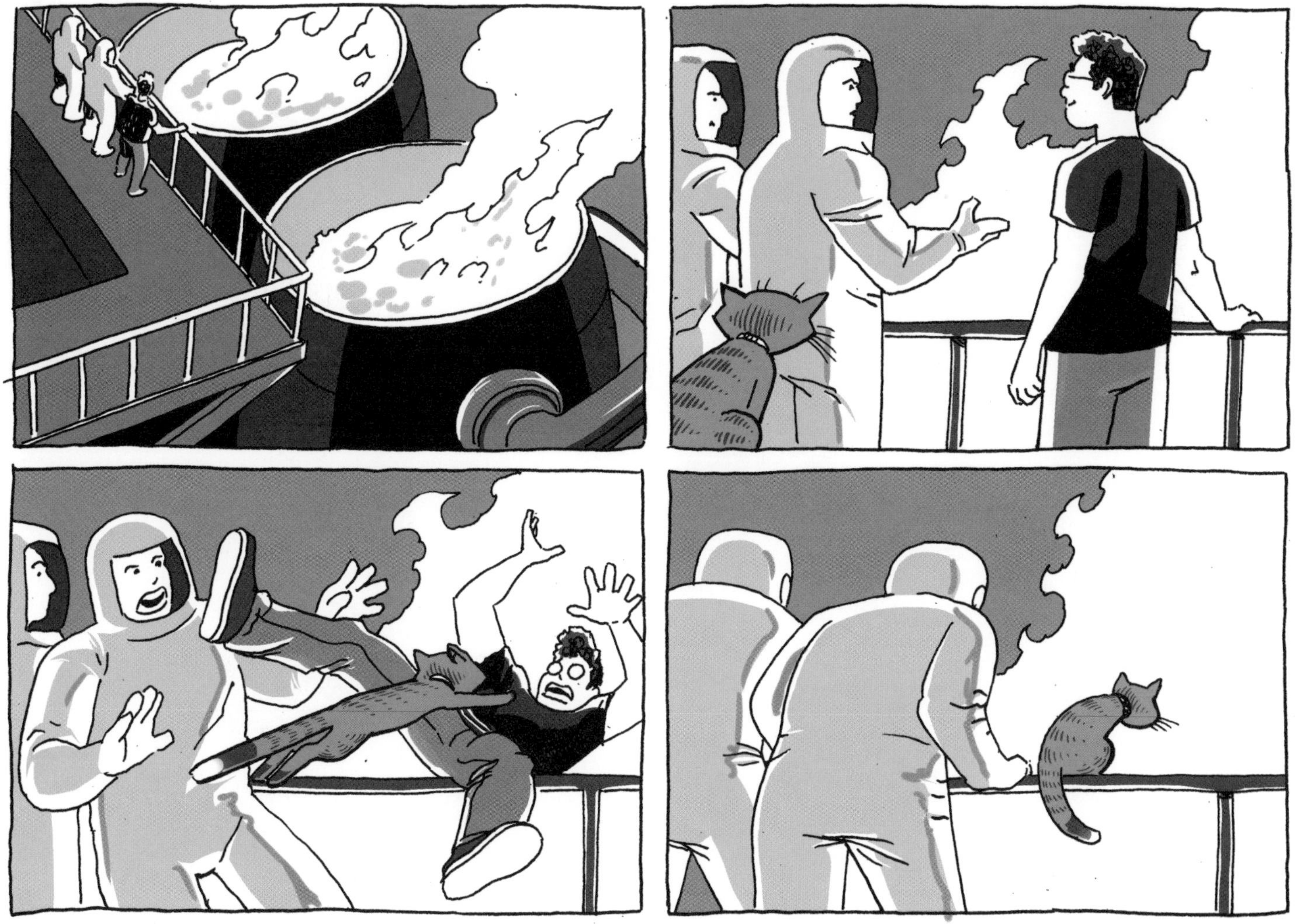

TIME FLIES

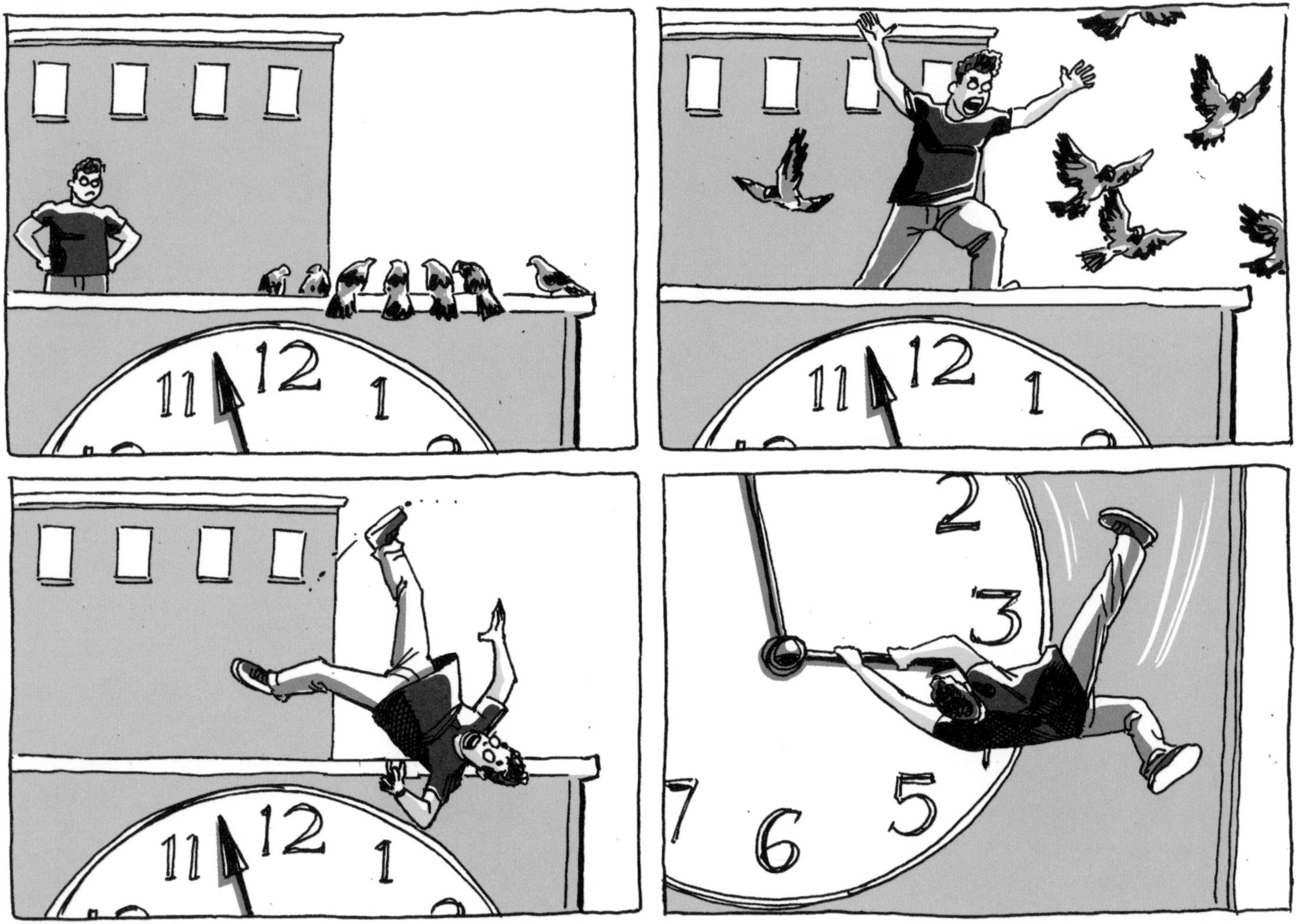
11
12
1
11
12
1
11
12
1
2
3
5
6
7

WHY DID IT HAVE TO BE CLOWNS?

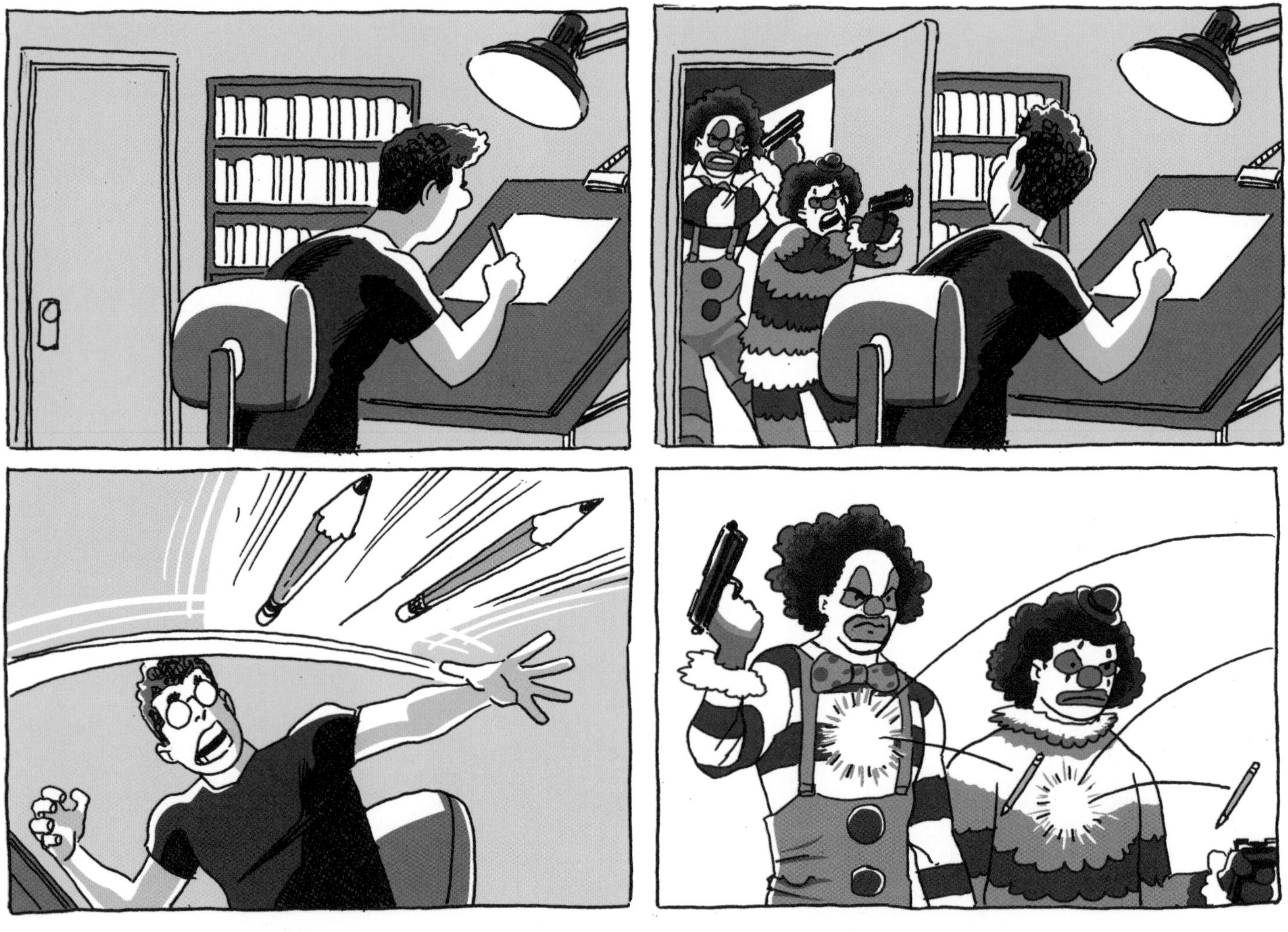

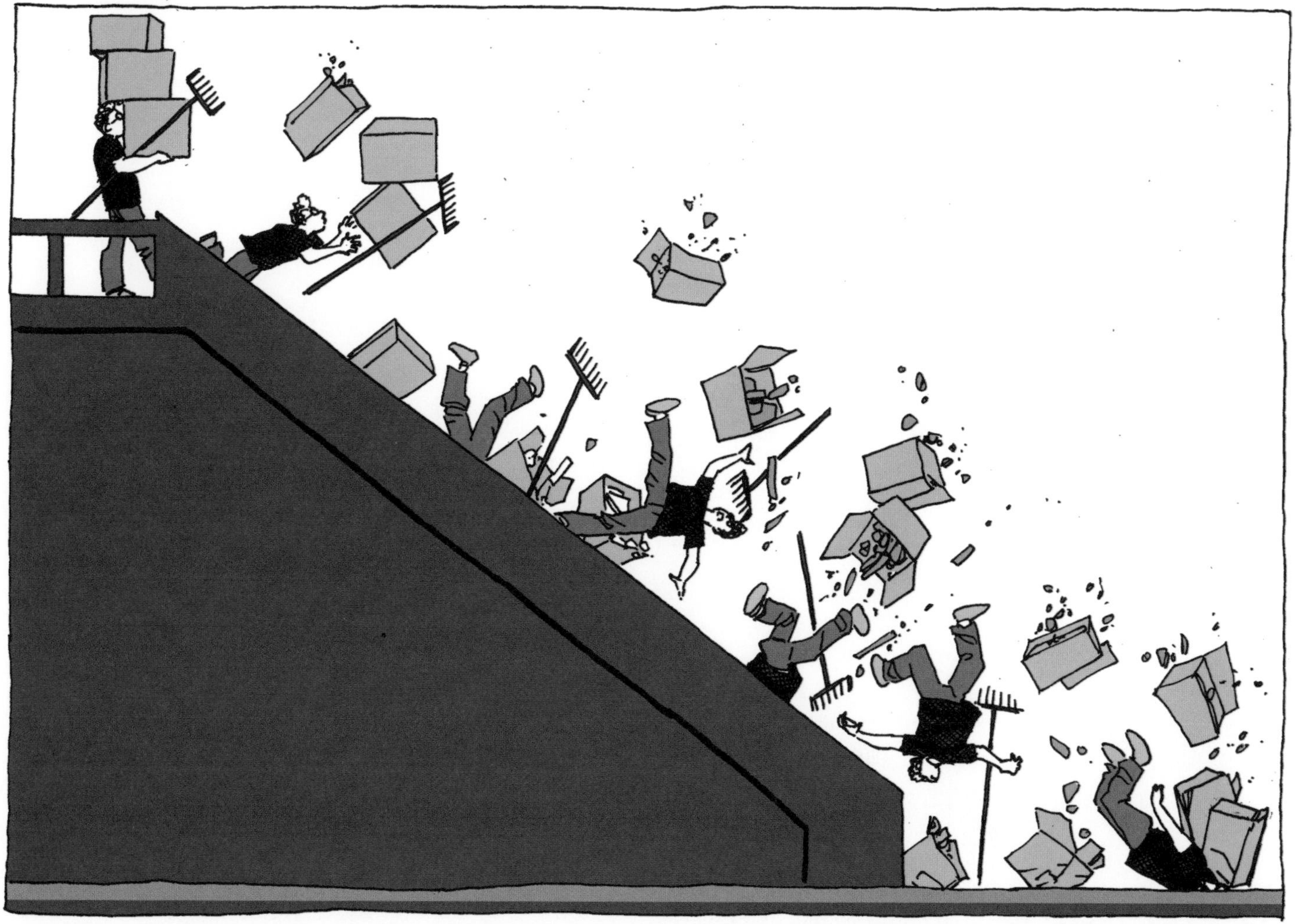

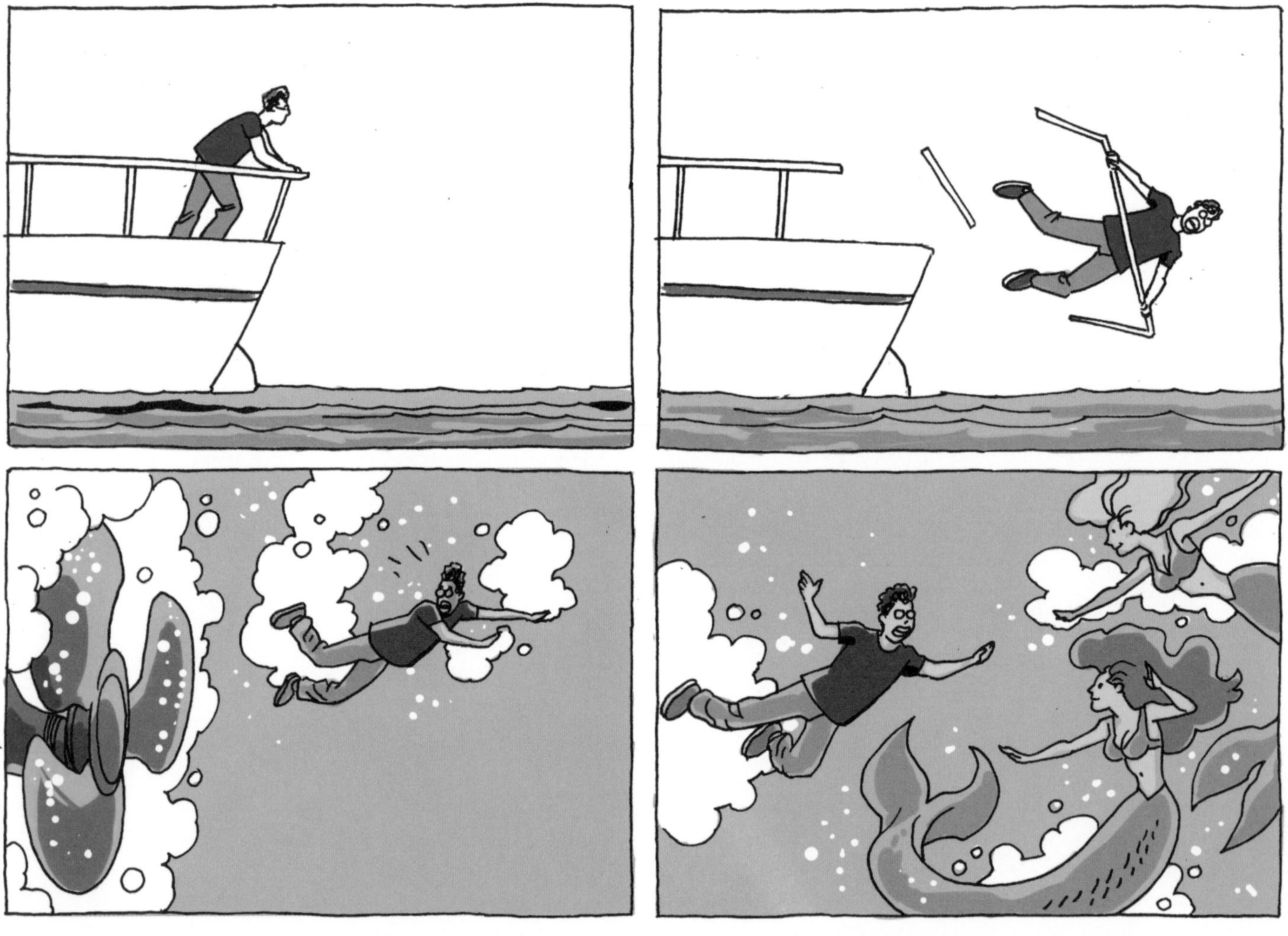

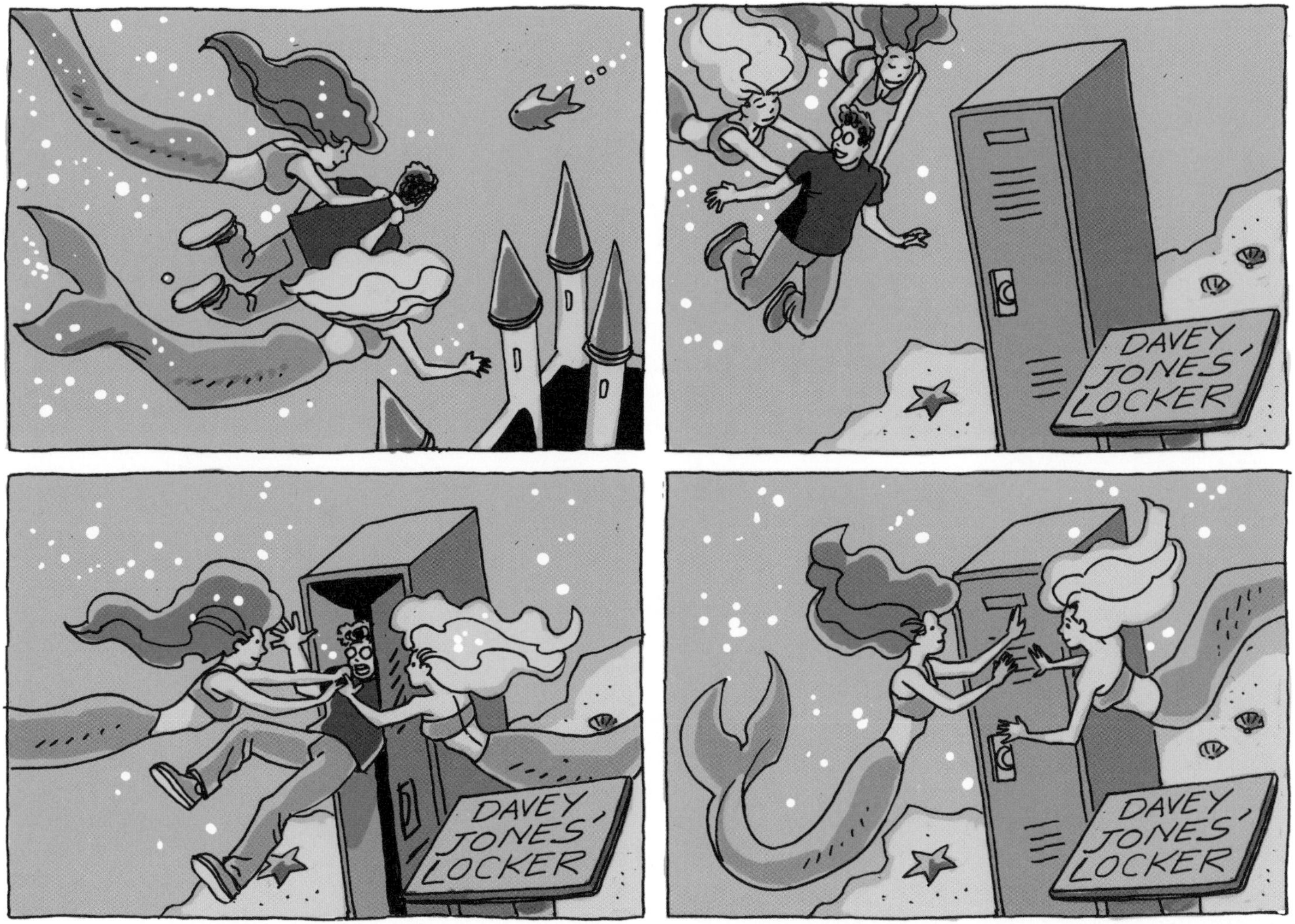
DAVEY JONES' LOCKER
DAVEY JONES' LOCKER
DAVEY JONES' LOCKER

THE FRIENDLY GHOST

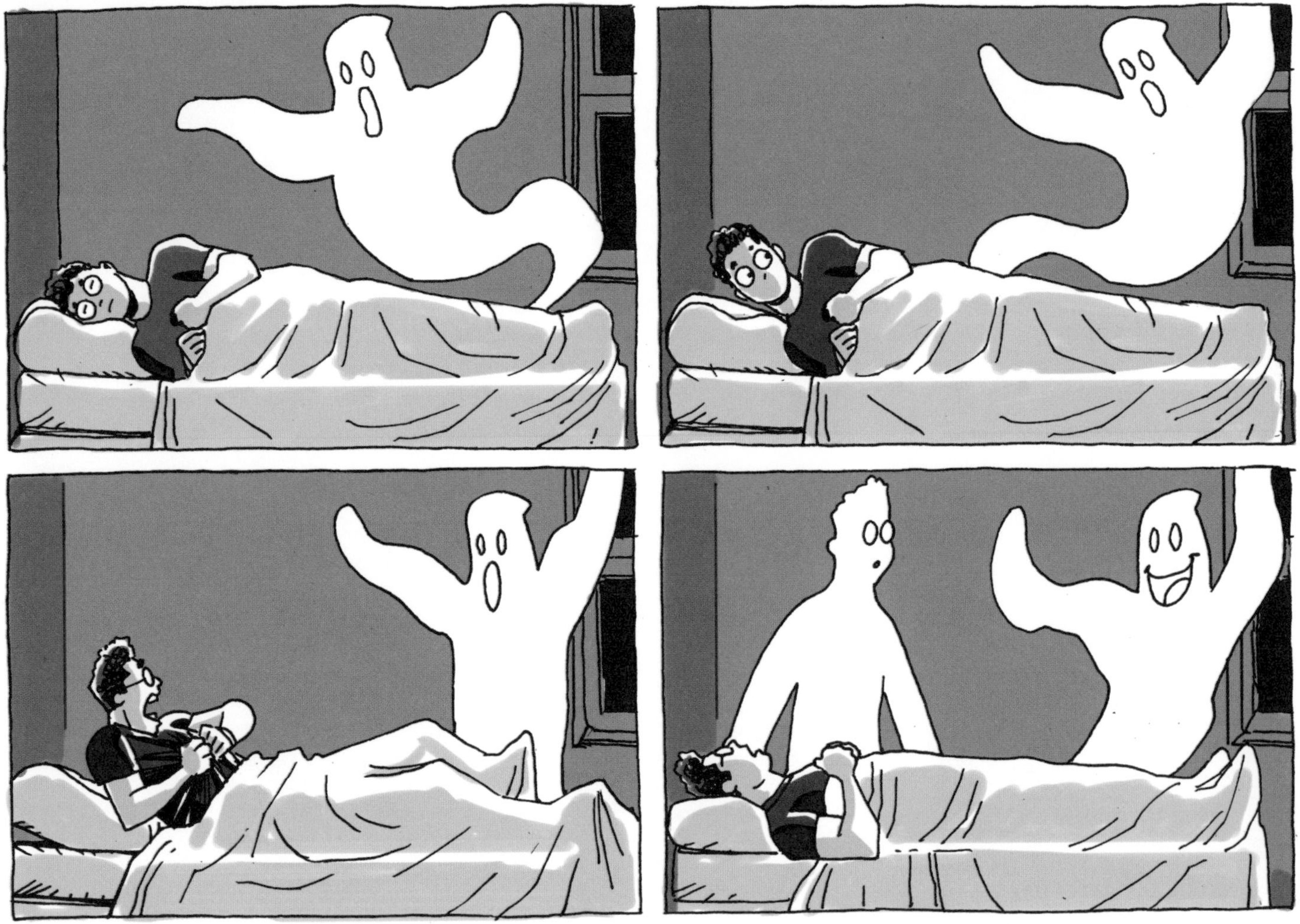

MAKE A WISH

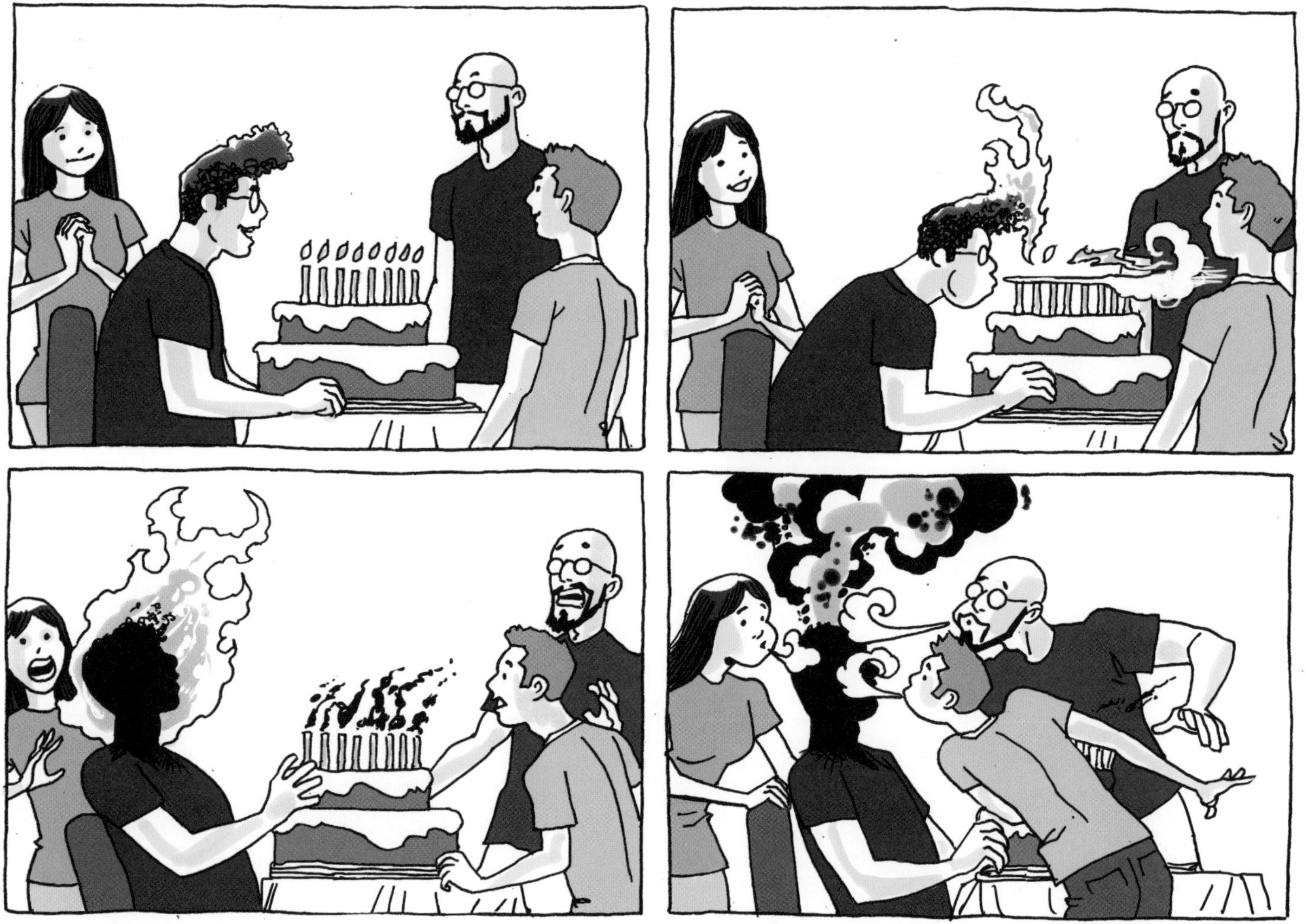

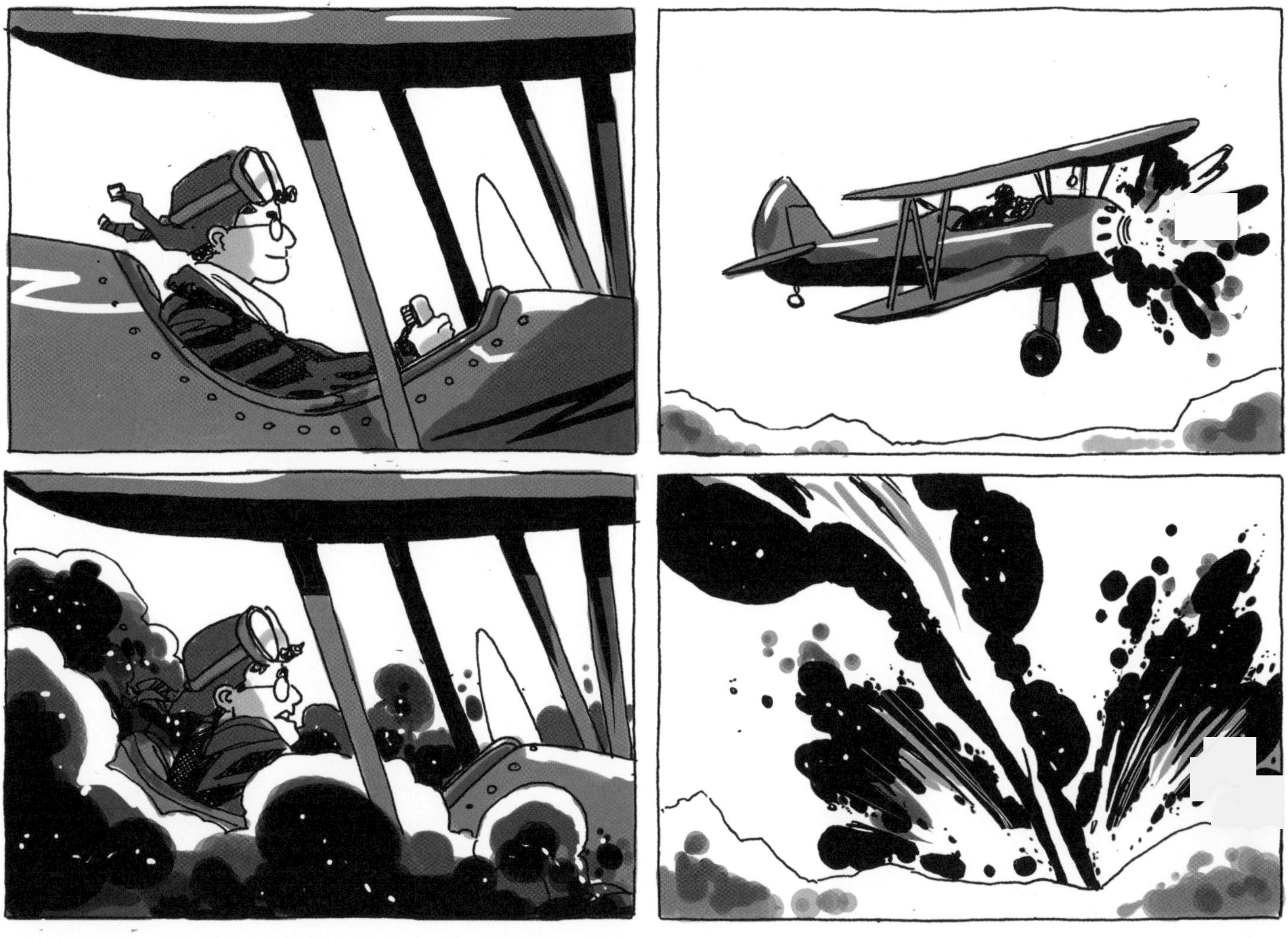

S.O.S.

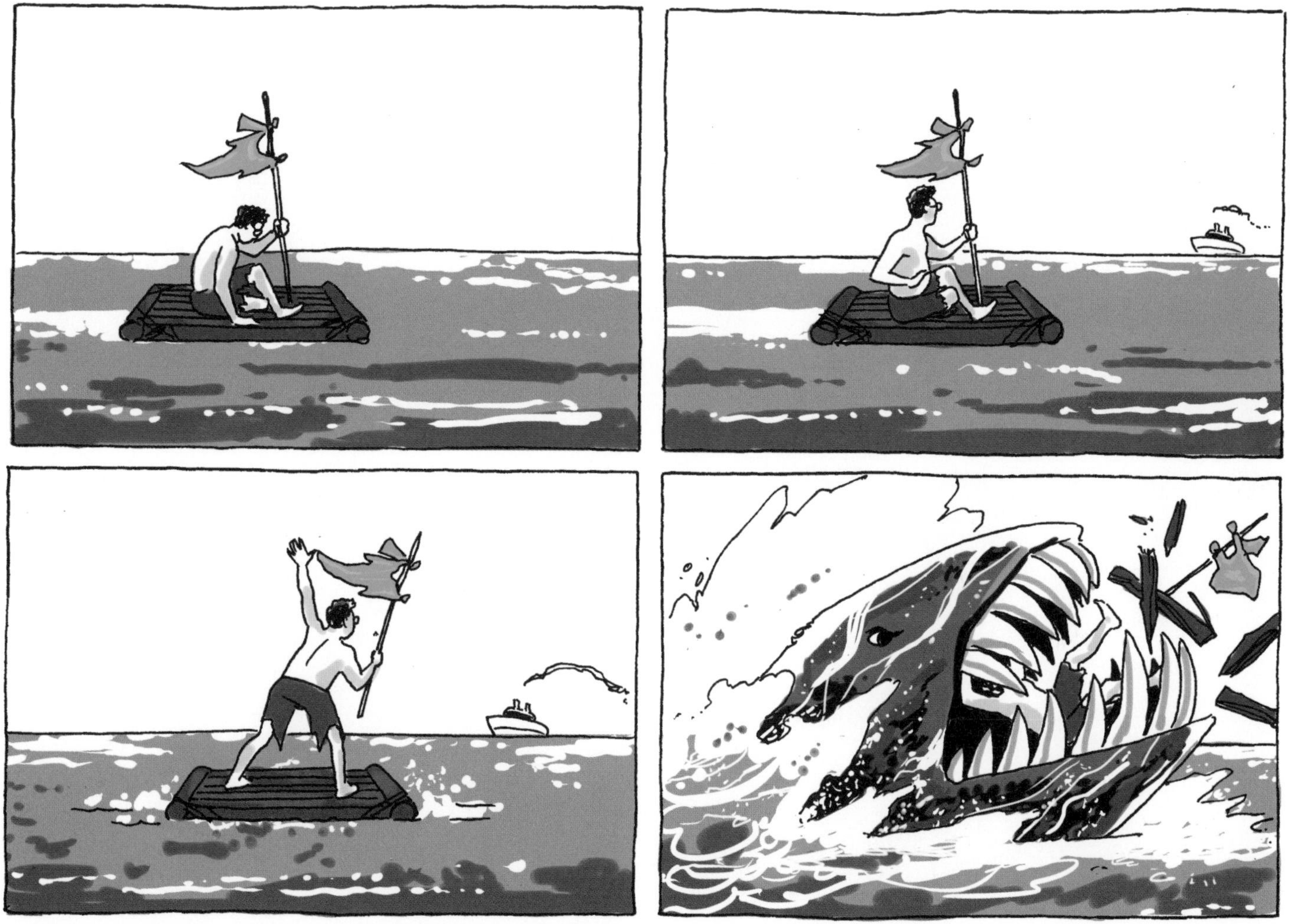

PUBLICATION DAY

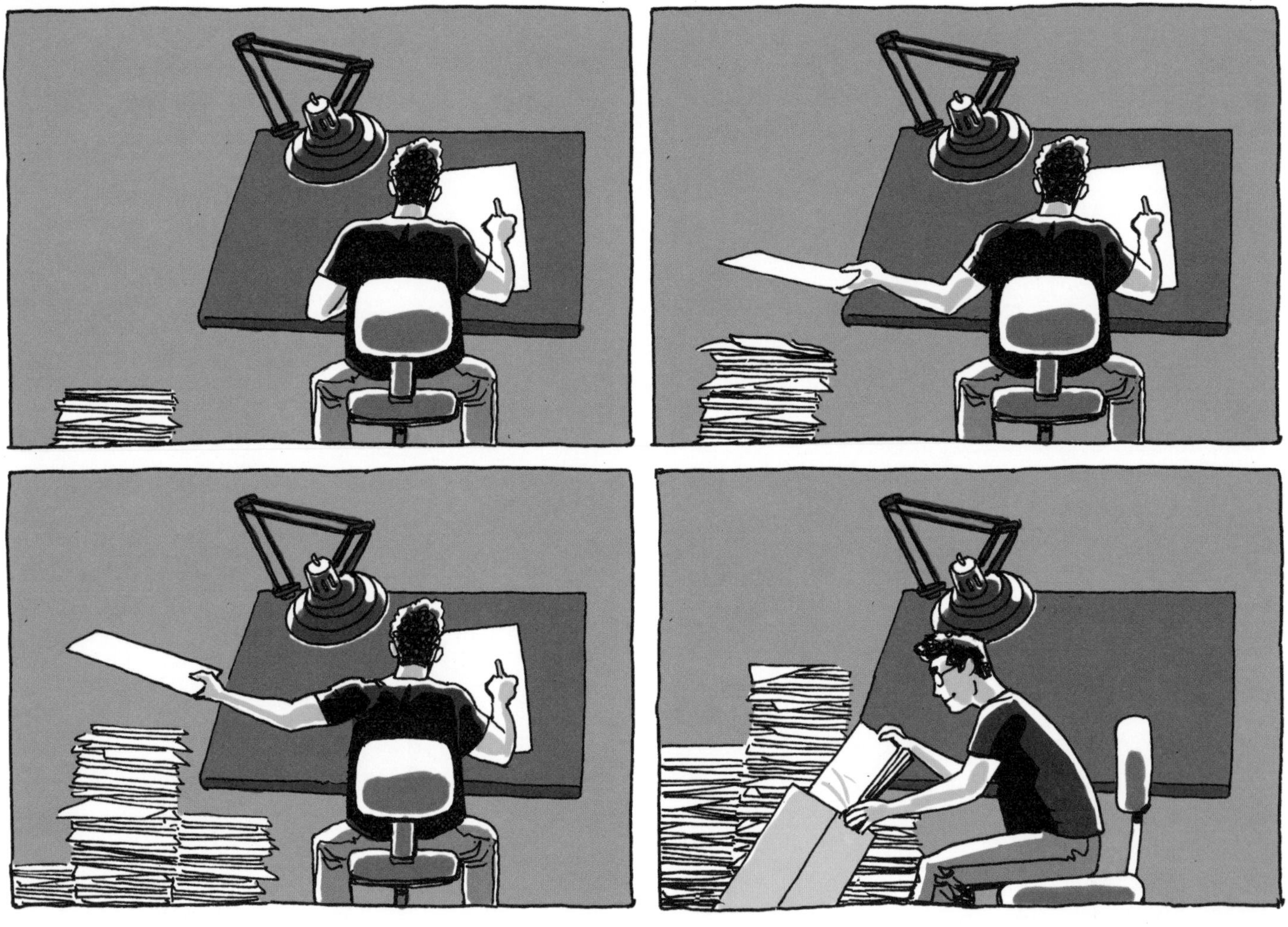

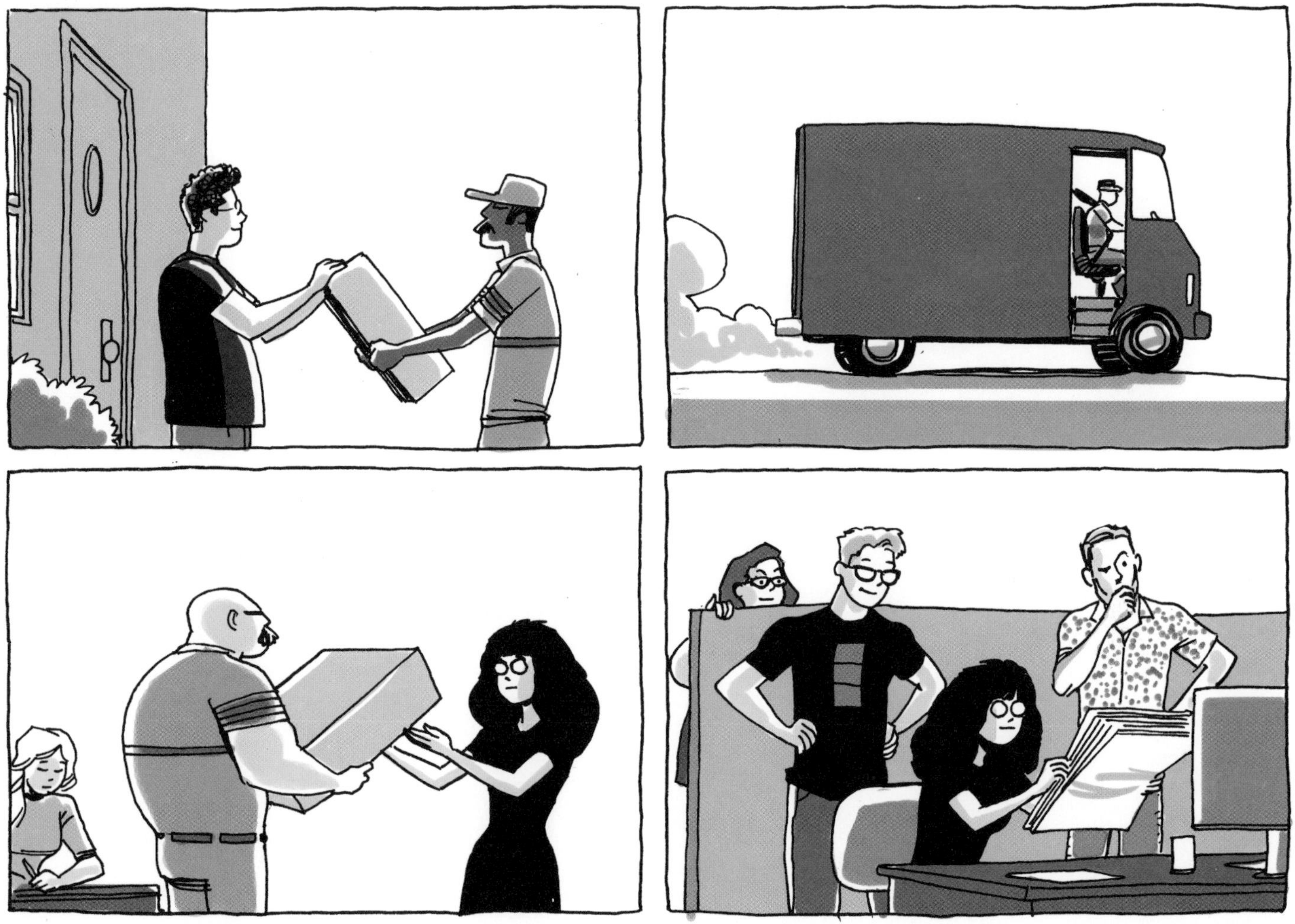

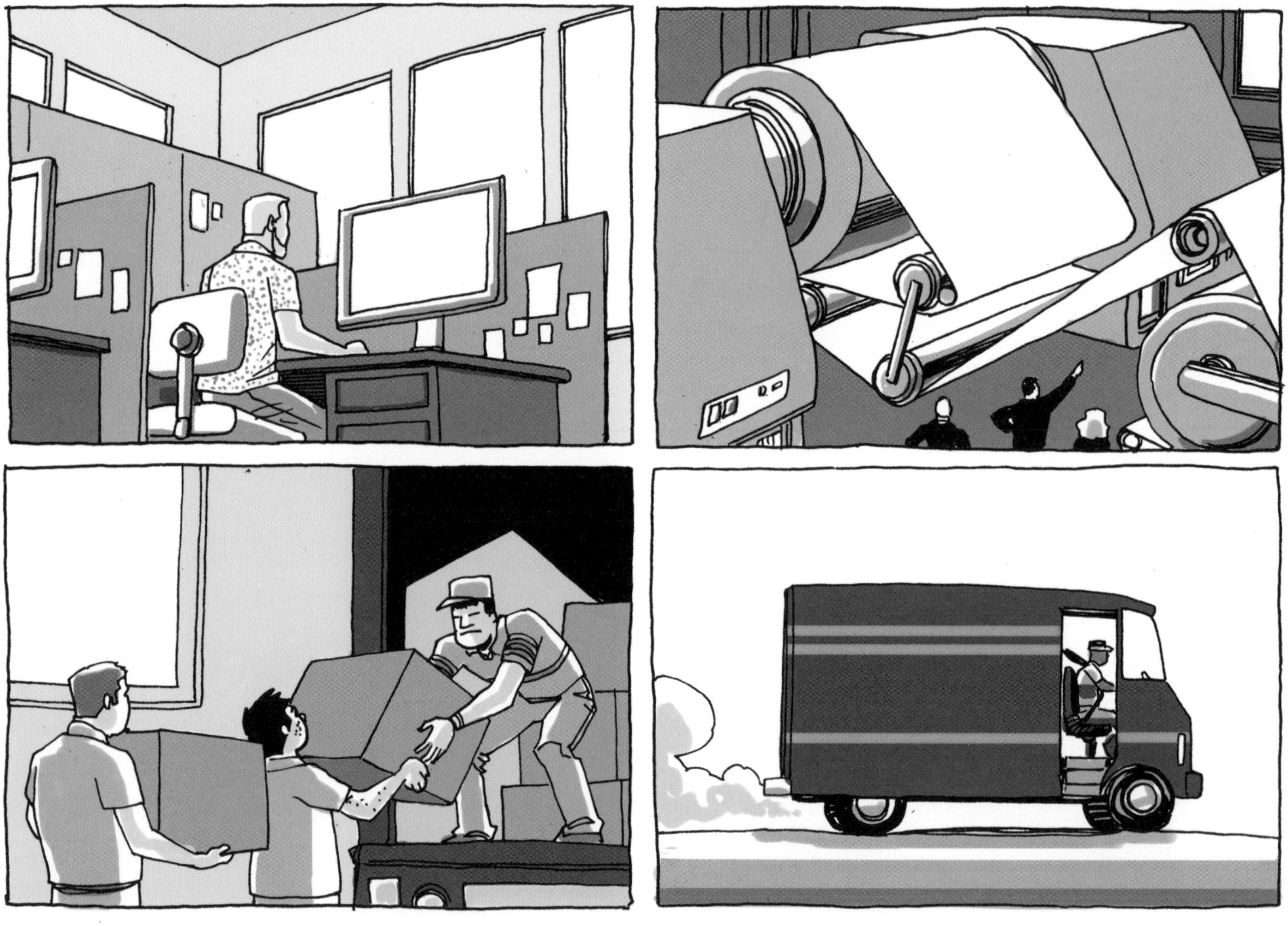

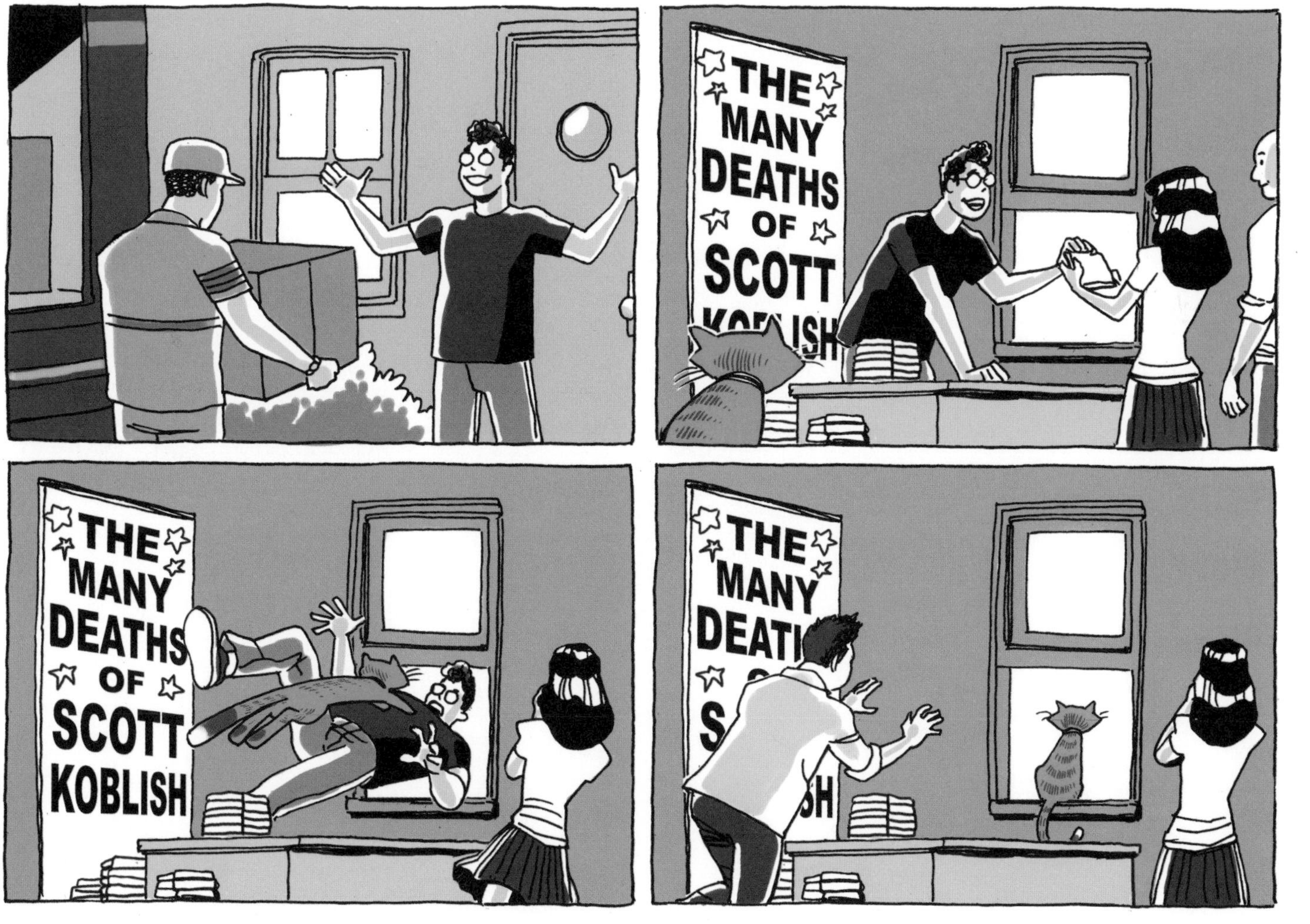
THE MANY DEATHS OF SCOTT
THE MANY DEATHS OF SCOTT KOBLISH
THE MANY

ACKNOWLEDGMENTS

To Violet, James, Mom (Kelly), and Katie—my eternal thanks for all you have done to make this book a reality. I am clumsy at expressing myself through words, and I owe you all more than I can ever say. Special thanks to the amazing folks at Chronicle Books, Steve, Michael, April, Beth, and Lia, my eternal thanks for all your hard work.

ABOUT THE AUTHOR

SCOTT KOBLISH is an Eisner-nominated cartoonist, *Guinness Book of World Records* holder, and artist who has worked on more than 500 comic books, including titles such as *Deadpool*, *Spider-Man*, *Captain America*, and *Thor*. For many years, he has also been drawing his own death for his own amusement. He lives in Los Angeles.